**"You're certainly no gentleman, Rick McGill,"
Martha Ann said with feigned outrage.**

"No, I'm not, and I don't intend to be. Re-member that."

"Have you no scruples?"

"No. Do you?"

"Of course."

Moving with the ease of a predator who was sure of his quarry, he pulled her into his arms. "Let's see how many scruples you have, Mrs. Lucky O'Grady."

Her mouth was as soft and lush as he knew it would be. He took his time kissing her, waiting out the initial resistance, stoking the fires he knew were there. They weren't long in coming. When Martha Ann Riley heated up, she did it with style. He was going to enjoy this case—if he lived through it. As her mouth continued to move under his, he knew that uncovering her secrets was going to be exciting . . . and dangerous, too.

"Just as I thought," he said. "The lady is not a lady after all." He bent over to kiss the beauty mark above her lip.

"Stop doing that," Martha Ann said.

"When you stop liking it, I will. . . ."

WHAT ARE *LOVESWEPT* ROMANCES?

They are stories of true romance and touching emotion. We believe those two very important ingredients are constants in our highly sensual and very believable stories in the *LOVESWEPT* line. Our goal is to give you, the reader, stories of consistently high quality that may sometimes make you laugh, sometimes make you cry, but are always fresh and creative and contain many delightful surprises within their pages.

Most romance fans read an enormous number of books. Those they truly love, they keep. Others may be traded with friends and soon forgotten. We hope that each *LOVESWEPT* romance will be a treasure—a "keeper." We will always try to publish

LOVE STORIES YOU'LL NEVER FORGET
BY AUTHORS YOU'LL ALWAYS REMEMBER

The Editors

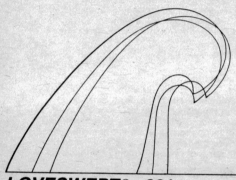

LOVESWEPT® • 381

Peggy Webb
Valley of Fire

BANTAM BOOKS
NEW YORK • TORONTO • LONDON • SYDNEY • AUCKLAND

VALLEY OF FIRE

A Bantam Book / February 1990

LOVESWEPT® and the wave device are registered
trademarks of Bantam Books, a division of
Bantam Doubleday Dell Publishing Group, Inc.
Registered in U.S. Patent
and Trademark Office and elsewhere.

If you would be interested in receiving protective vinyl
covers for your Loveswept books, please write to this address
for information:

Loveswept
Bantam Books
P.O. Box 985
Hicksville, NY 11802

ISBN 0-553-44012-8

Published simultaneously in the United States and Canada

Bantam Books are published by Bantam Books, a division
of Bantam Doubleday Dell Publishing Group, Inc. Its trademark, consisting of the words "Bantam Books" and the
portrayal of a rooster, is Registered in U.S. Patent and
Trademark Office and in other countries. Marca Registrada.
Bantam Books, 666 Fifth Avenue, New York, New York 10103.

PRINTED IN THE UNITED STATES OF AMERICA

OPM   0 9 8 7 6 5 4 3 2 1

Prologue

"Martha Ann! Where are you?"

"I'm in the basement, roller-skating. Come on down, Evelyn."

Martha Ann stuck out her arms for balance and tried to stop. It didn't work. The skates kept on rolling. She probably would have rolled straight through the wall if she hadn't run into the sofa. She banged her shins against the sofa frame and landed bottom up on the cushions.

That's how her sister found her when she came down the basement stairs.

"For goodness sakes, Martha Ann. What in the world are you up to now?"

Martha Ann righted herself, smoothing down her dark hair and her white shorts at the same time.

"I'm learning to roller-skate. I never did get the hang of it when we were kids." She patted the seat beside her. "Come sit down."

Heaving a great sigh, Evelyn sat beside her older sister. "Next thing I know you'll be taking up something dangerous, like race car driving."

"Not yet. But I'm only thirty-seven. There's still plenty of time."

Evelyn let out another big sigh. It wasn't lost on Martha Ann. She'd watched Evelyn struggle through four years of a nightmare married to a man who gambled away every penny they had, working like a Trojan at her little clothing store in Pontotoc, trying to pay the rent and keep food on the table. And now Evelyn was pregnant.

The Riley girls never did have any sense when it came to men.

Martha Ann leaned down and took off her roller skates. Putting variety into her life could wait. Her sister needed her. "Tell me about it, Evelyn."

"Lucky's gone again. I found this note when I got up this morning."

She held a small scrap of paper toward her sister. "Sweetie Pie," it said, "I hear the big one calling my name. Be back when I win a pot full."

Martha Ann folded the note and handed it back to her sister.

"Where do you think he's gone this time?"

"I have no idea. All I know is that I love him."

Martha Ann stood up and began to pace. "Well, gambling's not legal in Mississippi, so that means he's either found an illegal game or he's out of the state. The last time he went to Florida. Of course, the racing season is over, but still there's the lottery and jai alai." She stopped pacing and looked down at her sister. "How much money did he take?"

"I don't know. I haven't had time to check."

"You can do that this afternoon, and while you're at it, see if he called any travel agencies."

Evelyn pushed off the sofa, using the arm for support. Folding her hands over her protruding abdomen, she faced her sister.

"What are you thinking?" she asked Martha Ann.

"I'm going to find that husband of yours. Then I'm going to bring him back and hog-tie him to his bed. He's going to be around when he becomes a father, and furthermore, he's going to enroll in Gamblers Anonymous."

For the first time that day, Evelyn smiled. Martha Ann knew her sister thought she was brilliant and intrepid and resourceful. And although sleuthing was about as far from teaching history at a junior college as you could get, her sister's faith in her never wavered. Evelyn trusted her to find Lucky and bring him home.

The Riley girls had one thing in common—they never gave up.

"What about school, Martha Ann?"

"I have two weeks before I start teaching the summer session. Don't worry."

"But I do. I can't help myself." Evelyn snapped open her purse and took out her car keys. "Tell me one thing before I go. How do you propose to find my husband?"

"I'll think of something."

One

Rick McGill leaned back in his cane-bottomed swivel chair, propped his feet on his scarred desk, and sipped warm orange soda straight from the bottle. His feet sent an untidy pile of papers skittering across his desk, but he didn't bother to pick them up. It was too hot. Sweat rolled down the side of his face and dampened the front of his open-neck shirt. The ancient air conditioner in the corner of his office did its best, but it was no match for the heat.

Outside his window he could see heat waves radiating from the streets of Tupelo. Not even the mellow voices of the Lennon Sisters crooning over station WOLD could take his mind off the heat. The weatherman had said it was ninety-five degrees, and that had been at eight o'clock in the morning. He'd bet it was a hundred and five by now.

He tipped up the bottle and took another swig of soda. Just as he was taking the bottle from his lips, a limousine rolled down Broadway and stopped in front of his office. A uniformed driver got out of the car and opened the back door. Out stepped the most stunning woman Rick had ever seen. She was wearing a white suit cut in the style of the forties. The tight skirt set off the finest pair of legs he'd seen since he'd met that cancan dancer out in Oklahoma, and the flirty peplum bounced around hips that could make a man give up orange pop. She was wearing a hat too—an honest-to-goodness hat with a sassy little veil that didn't quite hide the bow-shaped mouth and the glossy black hair.

And she was coming up his sidewalk. Fate was smiling on him today.

He set the soda bottle on the desk and watched his front door. When she came through, she stood a moment, one hand on her fine hips, the other draped artfully on the door frame.

By george, she was posing. Rick leaned further back in his chair and drawled, Humphrey Bogart style, "Anything I can do for you, sweetheart?" He loved games. If she wanted to be Betty, he'd be Bogey.

When she smiled, he noticed the beauty spot just above her lips. It looked real, but he couldn't be sure.

"I'm looking for a man." The woman left the doorway and walked dramatically into the room.

She smelled like money: The rich smell of Italian leather, the clean smell of real silk, the elegant smell of expensive perfume. She looked like money too. She wore a square-cut diamond ring on her left hand and a bracelet of baguettes on her right wrist, the real McCoys if he wasn't mistaken—and he rarely was.

"Then you've come to the right place." He moved his feet off the desk, taking his time. "I'm the best private investigator in Tupelo."

"So I've heard." Martha Ann Riley folded her hands

in her lap so the rented diamonds would catch the sun coming through the window and shine in his eyes. She held her back straight and tried not to sweat on the borrowed silk suit. Then she crossed her legs and began to swing the left one, delicately, as she figured a lady of class and distinction would, the toe of the Italian leather high heels pointing straight at him.

The shoes were hers.

"You *are* Rick McGill, aren't you?"

"At your service." He inclined his head with just the right amount of acknowledgment but absolutely no deference. His reputation had been built on arrogance and daring. He wanted to keep it that way. "What can I do for you, Miss . . ."

"Mrs." She watched his face fall. Too bad, she thought. It was such an interesting face, lean and craggy and full of humor. The way her luck ran, though, he'd turn out to be a thief like her ex-husband or a scoundrel like her last boyfriend. Altogether, it was best if she pretended to be married. "Mrs. Lucky O'Grady." She used her sister's title without a twinge of conscience. It was all for a good cause.

"Lucky?"

"That's his real name. Honest to goodness."

"And you are . . ."

"I've told you my name."

"No. You've told me your husband's name. If I take you as a client, I'll need to know yours."

"Why?"

"Saves time. If we get into a tight situation, I can hardly take the time to say, 'Duck, Mrs. Lucky O'Grady.' Now can I? By the time I got all that out of my mouth you could be dead."

She briefly considered using her sister's name,

but decided she might forget to answer to it. "My name is Martha Ann, but I can tell you, Mr. McGill—"

"Rick."

"—Lucky is hardly the type of man who goes around carrying a gun."

"You never know."

He stared boldly at her in a way that would have insulted her if he'd been an ordinary man. But she'd long since decided this Rick McGill was no ordinary man. He was the dangerous type who could say or do anything and make a woman like it. Men like that had always attracted her. It was a darned good thing she'd decided on this charade.

"Not Lucky. All I want to do is find him, not get into a shoot-out with him."

"You've already proved my point."

"What point?"

"That you never know about people. If this Lucky O'Grady was fool enough to leave a woman like you, he'd do anything."

"I suppose I should say thank you."

"You're welcome."

"Will you take my case?"

"It depends."

"On what?"

"On whether I'm interested and whether you can pay my exorbitant fee."

Martha Ann had only two weeks to find Lucky, and then she had to be back at school. If she couldn't hire Rick McGill, she didn't know where she would turn. Anyhow, she wanted him and no one else. She'd done some checking before coming to Tupelo to see him. He was a flamboyant adventurer, an oil field fire fighter turned private investigator who se-lected his cases the way a jeweler would a fine diamond. Although his life-style was extravagant, he took very few cases. Talk was that he had a private source of income. Some people said it was Texas oil, others said Colombian emeralds, and a few even said gambling casinos and whorehouses.

He was just the kind of man she wanted. Finding her sister's husband was her primary concern, but she planned to have a grand adventure while she was searching. She figured if she was going to spend the money she'd saved for her trip to Europe on finding Lucky, she might as well have a blast.

She leaned forward and provocatively wet her lips. At the same time she made sure her borrowed skirt inched a little higher up her legs. She wasn't above flirtation to get what she wanted. And she wanted Rick McGill. Professionally speaking, of course.

"How can I make you interested, Rick?"

"By pulling down your skirt, for starters. I don't fool around with married women."

She stood up so fast, her hat slid down over one ear. "Good day, Mr. McGill."

"Not so fast."

She heard his chair bang to the floor as she marched toward the door. She was almost through it when he caught her shoulders and spun her back around.

"Just a minute, Miss High-and-Mighty O'Grady. We have unfinished business."

"We have no business, Mr. McGill."

"You came to me, remember?"

The face she'd thought so full of humor had changed. He looked like a fierce hawk as he stared down at her.

"A decision I sincerely regret."

"What about Lucky?"

He had her there. She'd just have to swallow her pride.

"Does that mean you're taking the case?"

"Any woman who can fill out a silk suit the way you can has my undivided attention."

She gave him a triumphant smile. "I thought you didn't fool around with married women."

"I don't. But that doesn't keep me from enjoying the view."

"You can turn loose my shoulders now."

"You won't try to flee?"

She tipped her head back, righting her dashing little hat as it threatened to slide off her head.

"I never make promises, Rick."

"Then we understand each other. Neither do I."

He let go of her and went back to his battered desk.

She followed him into the room and sat back down in her chair.

"I assume money is no object with you, Martha Ann."

That's precisely what she had wanted him to assume.

"No," she lied.

"Good. Now that the fee is out of the way . . ."

"Could you give me a ballpark figure?" His eyebrows went up. "My CPA, you know. He's a stickler for this sort of thing. Has to know the exact price tag on every little old diamond I buy."

"Five thousand a week, plus expenses. Half is refundable if I don't deliver."

She wanted to die right there in the chair, just scoot down to the floor and expire in mortification. Ten thousand dollars for two weeks, plus expenses. He probably ate steak and lobster every day and charged it to the account.

She bought time by carefully rearranging her hat. There was no backing out now. Evelyn had to have her husband. Anyway, she'd be along to make sure Rick McGill didn't have hundred-dollar dinners and put them on the tab. And there was always Las Vegas. She'd planned to supplement her savings by playing the tables. The fee he'd named was more than she'd counted on having to win, but if her luck held, she could do it.

"It's a deal," she said.

"Good. Now tell me about Lucky."

"Don't we have to sign contracts or something first?"

"I work only with verbal agreements. My word is my bond."

"Well . . ."

"If you prefer, we can seal the bargain."

"Seal the bargain?"

Rick chuckled. "Not the way you're thinking."

"How do you know what I'm thinking?"

"I can tell when a woman wants to be kissed. And Mrs. Lucky O'Grady, you want to be kissed."

"You are the most arrogant man I've ever met."

"I try. It brings in business." He stood up and came swiftly toward her. "Don't worry, Mrs. O'Grady. I'm not going to kiss you."

"Don't worry, Mr. McGill, I wouldn't let you if you tried."

He roared with laughter. "I like you, Martha Ann." Reaching down, he took her hand. "This is the way we'll seal the bargain—with a handshake."

"A gentleman's agreement, Rick McGill?"

"Precisely, Martha Ann O'Grady."

His handshake was strong and powerful and warm and refreshingly different from all the wimpy handshakes she'd endured at college receptions. She was sorry when he let go.

This time, he didn't move back to his chair. He perched on the edge of his desk, looking deceptively relaxed. In the last ten minutes, though, she'd learned to distrust that nonchalant posture of his. He was as fierce and predatory as a hawk, and just as swift to strike.

"Now, Martha Ann. Suppose you start by telling me why you think Lucky left and whether you have any idea where he might be."

"He left because he has wanderlust, and I know precisely where he is. He's in Las Vegas."

"You're sure?"

"Positive. He didn't bother to hide it. All I had to do was call the airport and the bus station. He took a bus." She smiled. "I've done most of your job for you. All I really need you for is to go along with me as a backup in case he's dealing with the criminal element and in case he needs a little more than friendly persuasion to come home."

"You want me to be your backup?"

"Exactly."

"I work alone. I'll go to Vegas and bring your Lucky home, and you will pay me. All quick and clean and easy."

"That's not the deal."

"Are you trying to tell me that you're part of the deal?"

"I'm not trying, I'm telling. I go with you."

"Never."

She stood up. "Then consider the gentleman's agreement canceled." She started toward the door.

"Wait."

He knew he would regret what he was about to do.

In fact, he already did. Almost. Why he should break the rules for her, he didn't know. She was a stunning, intriguing woman. True. But she was also married. And yet . . . there was something about her, some air of mystery that made him want to dig a little deeper.

He caught up with her again and turned her around. Tipping her face up with one finger, he stared at her. The beauty mark beside her lips *was* real. What a shame he'd never get to taste it.

"I've decided to break the rules for you." He held her face just long enough to memorize the feel of that silky skin; then he let her go. "You can go with me. But get one thing perfectly clear. I call the shots. I'm not your backup, and you will do precisely as I say."

"I don't make promises."

"You may not make promises, but you will take orders."

"When do we leave?"

"At first light tomorrow morning."

"Good. I'll pick you up in my car. The drive should take only three days, two if we push. It's cheaper than flying. We can take bedrolls—" Rick McGill burst into laughter. "What's so darned funny?"

"You be here at seven o'clock in the morning, Martha Ann. My plane will be ready."

"We're flying?"

"Yes. In my private plane, a twin engine Cessna." Her face went pale. "Unless you've changed your mind about going."

"I haven't changed my mind. I'll be here."

He stood at his window and watched her walk all the way out to the big black limousine. She was a luscious number that put all the other women he'd played around with in the shade. It would have been fun to have had a brief flirtation with her. Rick shook his head with regret.

As the car rolled down the street and out of sight, he decided that the Fates must still be watching out for him. He'd had a narrow escape with his last woman, Diane. She'd loved skydiving and cuddling and dancing to the golden oldies. And he'd come within an inch of falling in love with her. Falling in love didn't fit into his life-style. There were too many pretty women out there for him to consider settling down with one. He was only forty. He had years of fun left before he did anything as mundane as settle down.

He went back to his desk and sat down. Pulling out a pad of paper, he began to jot down notes. He wrote an exact description of his client, right down to the estimated price tag of the diamonds on her wrist and finger. Suddenly a part of their conversation replayed itself. "Give me a ballpark figure. . . . Driving is cheaper than flying." For somebody with all the trappings of wealth, she'd certainly been concerned with money.

With his notes in hand, he picked up the phone and dialed. What he'd told Martha Ann O'Grady about not working with contracts was absolutely true. He'd discovered that it was useless to ask for addresses and phone numbers, since most people seeking his help gave him false information anyway. If he wanted to know the truth about his clients, he had to find out for himself.

"Records," the voice at the other end of the line said.

Rick smiled. "Clinton, Rick McGill here. I need a favor."

"You always do, buddy. Shoot."

"What have you got on a Lucky O'Grady?"

Rick heard the sounds of the computer in the background. As Clinton began to talk, Rick began to smile.

By the time he'd hung up, he was laughing. Rolling his pencil idly between his fingers, he said aloud, "I do believe there's more to you than meets the eye, *Mrs.* Lucky O'Grady."

Two

"Well, how did it go?"

Evelyn turned toward Martha Ann as the rented limousine carried them down Broadway, past the courthouse, past the old Lyric Theater, past city hall. The powerful car engine hummed, and the efficient air-conditioning cooled the two women.

"Rick McGill took the case. We leave for Las Vegas in the morning."

Evelyn flung her arms around her sister. "How can I ever thank you."

"By smiling."

Evelyn leaned back in the seat, snuffled loudly, took her handkerchief out of her purse, and blew her nose, then gave Martha Ann a watery smile.

"How's that?"

"That's more like it. And I intend to see that you do nothing but smile from now on. When I bring that husband of yours home, he'll turn into the finest family man in northeast Mississippi."

"How much is it going to cost you, Martha Ann?"

"Don't worry about that."

"But I do. You're not rich, and Lord knows, I don't have any money. I hear these private investigators don't come cheap."

"I have some money saved."

"But is it enough?"

Martha Ann gave her sister an impish grin. "I know how to turn it into a fortune."

"Martha Ann! You're not planning on gambling."

"I practically put myself through college doing it. I can do it again."

"Lord, but that was nearly twenty years ago."

"Don't say it. You make me feel old."

"I'll pay you back, Martha Ann. Every penny. I promise."

"You will not."

"Yes, I will. I can't let you do this otherwise."

"I'm doing it because I love you . . . and I owe you, Evelyn."

"Don't start that again."

"I feel responsible."

"You couldn't help that I fell in love with Lucky."

"Yes, but I introduced you. I knew he was a gambler; I even suspected he had a problem. And yet I introduced that scoundrel to my baby sister."

"It was because I begged and pleaded. It was 'Lucky this and Lucky that.' Every time you came home from that school where the two of you taught, you had another exciting story to tell about Lucky. Living out on the desert in that drab little house, watching Mom try to hang on to that little ranch after Dad died, I thought Lucky O'Grady was the most exciting man in the whole wide world." She sniffed and blew her nose again. "I still do. Oh, Lord, I love him, Martha Ann."

She leaned her head on her sister's shoulder and began to sob.

Martha Ann wrapped her arms around Evelyn and crooned to her as if she were a baby. "Go ahead and cry. Let it all come out. I'll bring him home. I promise."

It took twenty minutes to get from Tupelo to Pontotoc to drop off Eveyn, and another hour for Martha Ann to get back home to Fulton. She paid the limousine driver, then got into her own reliable Honda Civic and returned the rented diamonds and the borrowed clothes.

When she got back to her own modest house within walking distance of Itawamba Community College where she taught, she began to pack. She had no idea what sort of things she would need on her trip, but she believed in being prepared. She put in jeans and cool cotton blouses and sturdy walking shoes and a sweater. Even in the summertime she knew how cool the desert could be at night. After all, she'd grown up there.

Next she packed her slinky black silk skirt and three brightly colored silk blouses—a fire engine-red one, a shocking purple one, and a neon-blue one. They weren't all that fancy, but the beading she'd stitched onto the shoulders gave them a little pizzazz. Men didn't usually know that much about clothes. She figured her homemade frocks looked good enough to fool Rick McGill.

She was determined to keep up her charade of being a wealthy married woman looking for her husband. She didn't want Rick to get scared that she couldn't pay the bills and then back out. And she certainly didn't want to fall for a man whose background might include gambling and no telling what else.

She thought of the way he had looked when he'd caught her by the shoulders. Powerful. She'd felt the power oozing from his body. She shivered. It was safer to keep pretending to be Mrs. Lucky O'Grady. Anyhow, she was enjoying her role. It added a little spice to her life.

Last of all she packed her rosary. She had been born a Methodist, but had taken the Catholic faith when she'd married Marcus Grimes. She guessed if Marcus hadn't been caught embezzling and sent to prison, she'd still be married to him, going to early mass and praying for forgiveness for staying married to a man she didn't love.

The Rileys were like that. They never gave up. Of course, Fate had carried Marcus off to jail, and she'd gotten her divorce and moved to Mississippi and become an Episcopalian. There was something so wonderfully liberating about being an Episcopalian. Still, in a pinch she counted on her rosary. And heaven knew, she'd need it the next day.

She was scared to death of flying.

Rick Mcgill was waiting for her in front of his office. Unfortunately, he didn't look a bit less attractive than he had the day before. As a matter of fact, she thought, he looked even better. There was something about a man in a flight jacket that was exceedingly sexy.

Evelyn, sitting beside her in the limousine, let out a long low whistle. "Is that him, Martha Ann? My gosh, he looks like a blond Clark Gable." Evelyn leaned over her sister to get a better view. "No wonder you picked him out."

"I didn't pick him out for his looks, Evelyn. I researched his background and selected him because he's supposed to be good. Quit gawking." She dug into her purse and pulled out a handful of bills. "This will pay for the limousine. I'll be in touch as soon as I can."

"Would you just look at those *legs* of his? You're liable to come back from Vegas with more than Lucky."

"Not if I can help it." Martha Ann turned to glance out the window at Rick McGill. He *did* look handsome in the early morning sun. She rolled her eyes heavenward. Lord, did you have to make him so delicious looking? she asked silently. Turning back to Evelyn, she gave her a quick hug. "Wish me luck."

"Good luck."

Martha Ann composed her face into just the right blend of aloofness and mystery and allowed the hired driver to help her from the car. He got her bags and delivered her to the sidewalk, where Rick was waiting.

"I'm glad to see you wore something sensible today." He assessed her with a boldness that made her believe he was seeing through her jeans and shirt, all the way to her black lace panties.

"Is that good morning, Mr. McGill?" Gracious, she thought, how his dark eyes danced when he looked at a woman. She managed a disgusted sniff, which was probably the best acting job she'd ever done. What she really wanted to do was drool and swoon. "If it is, your manners leave a lot to be desired."

"If you want formality and manners, you've come to the wrong place." He grinned at her. By george, she was good, he thought. He planned to enjoy this case to the hilt, starting right now. Reaching out, he patted her bottom. "Pick up your gear, sweetheart. It's time to get going."

He watched with amusement as she jumped out of his reach and feigned outrage. Picking up her suitcase, she glared at him. On her, the expression looked cute.

"You're certainly no gentleman, Rick McGill."

"No, I'm not, and I don't intend to be. Remember that."

"Yesterday you said you didn't fool around with married women."

"I've changed my mind."

"Have you no scruples?"

"No. Do you?"

"Of course."

Moving with the ease of a predator who was sure of his quarry, he took her suitcase and dropped it onto the sidewalk, then pulled her into his arms. He tipped her face up with one finger.

"Let's see how many scruples you have, Mrs. Lucky O'Grady."

Her mouth was as soft and lush as he knew it would be. He took his time kissing her, waiting out the initial resistance, stoking the fires he knew were there. They weren't long in coming. He felt the heat and sizzle of her all the way through his flight jacket. When Martha Ann Riley heated up, she did it with style. That long, lithe body sort of melted into his, and those delicious lips moved in magical ways.

He was going to enjoy this case, all right. If he lived through it. The enterprising beauty in his arms had already lied about her name, her wealth, and her marital status. What else was she lying about? As her mouth continued to move under his, he knew that finding out was going to be one of the most exciting things he'd done in a long, long time. And probably one of the most dangerous too. Just being in the same corner of the earth with a woman who kissed the way she did was dangerous.

Rick McGill loved danger. He courted it a moment

longer before letting her go; then he pulled back and smiled down at her.

"Just as I thought," he said.

"What?"

"This lady is not a lady after all."

The beauty mark above her lip looked fetching on her flushed face. He saw no reason to resist bending over to kiss it. So he didn't.

"Stop doing that," she said.

"When you stop liking it, I will." Grinning, he patted her bottom again. Then he picked up his suitcase and started toward the red Corvette parked beside the curb. "Let's go, sweetheart. I can tell you need that husband of yours."

What she needed was to have her head examined, Martha Ann thought as she picked up her own bag and followed him. Only her great loyalty to her sister kept her from turning around and going back to Fulton.

She watched as he tossed their bags into his car. Gracious, he was so appealing. She'd lied to herself, of course. It wasn't her great loyalty that drove her on: It was Fate. Here was an unscrupulous man who admitted that he was no gentleman and who'd proven it by kissing a married woman. Well, she wasn't really married, but that didn't count. Rick McGill was cut from the same cloth as Marcus Grimes and Bradley Lomax, the con man she'd dated last year. Dangerous men, all of them.

And she was fascinated.

Rick McGill drove his Corvette the way he did everything else, with reckless abandon. They whizzed through the streets of Tupelo so fast, Martha Ann didn't have much thinking time. It was just as well.

She'd already spent a night worrying about going up in a plane. All that time she should have been worrying about being alone with Rick McGill, wife chaser. And she couldn't pretend to herself that she hadn't liked that kiss. She had. Too much. Maybe she should tell him she was pregnant.

She just about resolved to add that lie to her charade when they arrived at the airport. The plane was every bit as bad as she had thought it would be. Sitting on the tarmac it looked too fragile to carry a flea across the country, let alone a scared woman and her unscrupulous companion.

"There she is." Rick gallantly opened her door and helped her from the car. His latent good manners hardly registered with her. "Isn't she a beauty?"

"I don't care if she's beautiful or not. What I want to know is will she stay in the air?"

His gaze swung from the plane to her. "You're not afraid, are you?"

"Who? Me?" She tossed her hair and jutted out her chin. "I'm not afraid of the devil."

His suppressed his grin. Her face was pale, and her blue eyes were wide with fright. He secretly admired the way she lied. "I didn't think so. Let's go."

Martha Ann climbed bravely into the cockpit and glanced out the window. The ground was still down there where it was supposed to be, and she wasn't doing anything to disgrace herself, like hyperventilating. But she'd packed a paper bag in her purse just in case.

She knew her fear of flying was ridiculous. And it was all Bud Jones's fault. Bud had been her college sweetheart, a good-looking ne'er-do-well whose passion had been stunt flying. One sunny day in April he'd persuaded Martha Ann to go up in his plane and witness his stunts firsthand. It hadn't taken much persuasion. In those days, flying hadn't bothered her, nor had anything else for that matter. She'd try anything.

She'd enjoyed having an up-close view of Bud doing his loops and rolls and dives. But suddenly the plane had stalled and gone into a spin. The earth had come toward them at a terrifying rate. All she'd thought of was how the choir would sound singing "Amazing Grace" at her funeral.

Bud had gotten them out of the spin somehow. But she'd never gone up in another plane. Until now.

She shut her eyes as the airplane engine roared to life.

"We're cleared for takeoff, Martha Ann. Here we go."

With her eyes still shut, she reached out blindly, clasped his arm, and nodded. She was obviously with a nut. Anybody who could be that cheerful when facing his own death had to be crazy.

Rick glanced down at the hand clutching his sleeve. The fingers were long and slim and tapered, the nails polished a pearly pink. He imagined how that hand would look on his bare chest, like a beautiful rose petal. He could hardly wait.

"Comfortable?" he shouted.

"Ummmhmmm."

He patted her hand, but she didn't even notice.

"Let me know if you need anything. Food, water, bathroom. I can set this baby down on a dime."

"I sincerely hope you don't have to."

He looked at her face. It was pale but gorgeous. The eyelashes were long and sooty, fanning down on cheeks he knew were soft as a soap bubble. Why was she so afraid of flying, he wondered. Of course, it was best not to worry about her fears. All he wanted to do was to find her sister's husband, collect his fee, and have a whale of a good time along the way. And from the small taste he'd had of Martha Ann Riley, she would certainly provide some first-class entertainment.

He chuckled as he thought of how easily he'd discovered her charade. It seemed that Lucky O'Grady wasn't that lucky after all. He'd been in enough gambling scrapes to be listed in the police computer. Nothing serious, just fines and plenty of aggravation for his family—Evelyn Riley O'Grady, his wife, five feet two, light brown hair, twenty-seven, owner of O'Grady's Dress Shop in Pontotoc; and his wife's sister, Martha Ann Riley, Ph.D., divorced, thirty-seven, five feet nine, hair as dark as a raven's wing, eyes the color of the sky at high noon, history professor at Itawamba Community College. The computer hadn't had all that about the raven hair and sky-blue eyes. He'd added those details himself.

His gaze raked over her body. There were plenty of other details he planned to add. But that would have to wait until they landed.

He turned his attention back to flying.

"Look, there's the Mississippi River," he said.

"Do I have to?"

"You're missing some beautiful sights."

"I can survive without seeing the world from ten thousand feet in the air."

"We're higher than that."

"Don't tell me. I don't want to know."

Martha Ann didn't know how she survived as far as Dallas, but she did. She even began to relax after they were on the ground again and having what Rick called a snack. He ordered a sixteen-ounce rib eye steak, rare, but she didn't complain. She'd willingly pay for champagne and caviar if that's what it took to keep him content until he got her safely on the ground in Las Vegas.

Back in the plane, she assumed her vigil with her eyes shut. Sometime later, when he remarked that they were flying over the Grand Canyon, she reached into her purse and felt for her rosary. Her lips began to move.

"What are you doing?" Rick asked.

"Saying my hail Marys."

"You're Catholic?"

"When the occasion calls for it."

She prayed from the Grand Canyon all the way to Lake Mead.

"Hoover Dam," Rick shouted.

"I don't want to know."

The desert stretched below them, wild and vast and beautiful. It was the kind of scene that made Rick aware of his own mortality. The rocks below them were millions of years old. What was the life of a man compared to the life of a mountain? he speculated. His petty strivings seemed insignificant compared to the magnificent grandeur of the land.

Suddenly, alarm rang through Rick's senses. Something was not right. The sounds and smells of the plane were out of kilter. He saw the plume of smoke at the same time he smelled the acrid scent of burning. His left engine was on fire. He shut off the fuel to that engine and scanned the ground below for a landing spot.

"Hang tight, Martha Ann. We're going in for an emergency landing."

Her eyes snapped open. "What?"

"Plane's on fire."

Her throat constricted, and her chest grew tight.

For an awful moment she thought she was going to faint. Then she looked at the man beside her. Rick McGill was as cool and in command as if he were strolling through the park on a Sunday afternoon. The sight of him miraculously calmed her down. For the first time since they'd begun the flight, she felt normal.

"What can I do?" she asked.

"As soon as we land, get out as fast as you can. Hit the ground running. Don't stop for anything." He turned to give her a thumbs-up sign. "We're going to make it, kiddo."

"You bet we will. Martha Ann . . . O'Grady never loses."

There was a valley coming up. He scanned the area, looking for the best spot. There it was, a long smooth canyon between two flat-topped bluffs. It looked wide enough. And long enough. Not a cloud in the sky. It was perfect, too perfect. The skin on the back of his neck prickled.

He felt the jolt when his wheels hit the rough terrain. The plane wobbled, its crippled engine trailing smoke; then it taxied to a stop.

Rick kicked open his door and literally dragged Martha Ann through. He didn't trust her to get out of the plane on her own. But she proved to be a trooper. She hit the ground running, just as he had instructed.

Holding her hand, he raced over the rocky canyon floor. She kept up with him, her long legs stretching out in a sprint.

They didn't stop until they reached a huge outcrop of rock that formed a natural cave. Pulling her with him, Rick ducked inside just as the explosion rocketed through the canyon.

"You okay, sweetheart?"

Her face was pale. "Your plane . . ."

"It's insured." Her teeth began to chatter. "Hey, it's all right. We're safe now." He wrapped his arms around her and pulled her close against his chest. She continued to shiver. "It's okay, baby. It's okay." He rubbed her back and began to rock her in a soothing motion. "Don't go into shock on me now, sweetheart. It's all over." She made a hiccuping sound against his shoulder. "Are you crying? Hey, don't cry. I'm here. I'll take care of you."

"I'm . . . not . . . cry . . . ing," she said between hiccups. "I always . . . do . . . this . . . when I'm . . . scared."

"There's a cure for hiccups." He tipped her face up with one finger and took possession of her lips.

This kiss was different from the first one, Martha Ann thought. There was a gentleness in his lips, a sweet tenderness that made her want to cuddle up to him forever. She responded by stepping closer and winding her arms around his neck. She rationalized her behavior by telling herself that the only way to cure her hiccups was to do it right.

Her hands crept up and tangled in the hair at the back of his neck. It was crisp and very masculine, yet wonderfully soft. She felt as if she had a handful of sunshine.

Rick dragged her closer, cupping her hips and moving them into his own. The kiss had long since ceased to be a cure for hiccups. He was kissing her for pure pleasure now. No need to kid himself, he thought. The woman in his arms was female dynamite, a seductive vamp who set his blood boiling.

His passion burst into full flower, and he groaned. Bending her over backward, he plunged his tongue between her teeth. The inside of her mouth was warm and silky and inviting. He explored it with the joy of a sailor on shore leave. His hips rocked against hers in a heady rhythm. His heart beat in a bongo-drum tempo.

When it was obvious to both of them that they couldn't keep kissing in the name of hiccups, they pulled apart.

Rick gave her a grin that was almost sheepish. "All cured now?"

"I think so."

"You only think so?" He reached for her. "In that case, we should continue the cure."

She backed out of his reach and held up her hand. "Please. I'm a married woman."

"How could I forget?" His chuckle echoed off the rock walls of the cave. "What do you say we explore our surroundings and figure a way out of our dilemma, Mrs. Lucky O'Grady?"

Three

"We're in the Valley of Fire."

Rick turned from his contemplation of the endless red bluffs and studied Martha Ann. They had been walking for ten minutes, and as far as he could tell there was nothing to distinguish this canyon from any other in the Southwest.

"How do you know?" he asked.

"I lived in this area once." She turned and pointed to a large section of sandstone atop an ancient bluff. "See that rock. What does it remind you of?"

"By george, it looks like a turtle."

"This entire valley is filled with such whimsical creatures. Nature's artwork. The result of millions of years of erosion cutting into the soft interbeds of the rock. And over there—" She pointed to a flat-faced rock that looked as if it had been varnished, shadings of blue and purple over red. Rick could barely make out the symbols carved into the rock. "Petroglyphs," she explained. "Carvings of the Ancient Ones who once lived in this valley."

Rick was fascinated—as much by her as by his

surroundings. She was a born teacher. It showed in the way her eyes lit up when she talked, the way her arms moved to encompass the valley, the animated lilt of her voice.

He smiled. For the moment, Martha Ann Riley had forgotten she was supposed to be a wealthy aloof married woman. He liked the real Martha Ann.

"How far are we from Las Vegas?"

"About fifty miles." Martha Ann lifted her face toward the sky. "It will be dark soon. We'd be foolish to try to walk out of the desert at night."

"I agree. We can surely find a shelter around here."

"Perferably one that isn't already occupied by a sidewinder."

"There are other things I'd rather cuddle up to."

Martha Ann thought of the cold desert night ahead with no blankets and no sleeping bags. She'd have only Rick McGill to keep her warm. As she watched him striding up the canyon, checking for a likely spot to sleep, she had plenty of time to fully appreciate her companion. He was lean and rangy and powerful. She'd be willing to bet that the kisses they'd exchanged were just a mere taste of the raw power of the man.

Unconsciously she shivered. It was going to be a long night.

Before they decided on a spot to camp, they dined on beans from the catclaw acacia. Water was no problem since the Valley of Fire was a tourist attraction, complete with water hydrants. It took them a while to find one, but when they did, they drank their fill.

"Martha Ann, if I have to be stranded in the desert, I'm glad it's with you." Rick polished off the last of his beans hungrily. "Who would have thought that a woman who doesn't have a worry in the world except the price of her next diamond would know what to eat in a desert?"

Was he teasing her, she wondered. He was laughing, but the look he gave her was a little too shrewd to be that of a man who believed everything he heard. She'd have to be more careful.

"Even rich people had to grow up somewhere. I suppose it's just a lucky coincidence that we crashed in my old stomping ground."

"Not so lucky." He got a faraway look in his dark eyes. "It never should have happened."

"How did it happen, Rick?"

A faulty fuel line leaking gasoline. The plane is thoroughly checked out before I fly, of course. Apparently the problem escaped detection. I'm sorry it happened, but it was no one's fault."

"You did an outstanding job of landing that crippled plane and keeping us from getting killed. I'm not placing blame."

"I know that, but you are certainly due an explanation. After all, you are paying me to take care of you."

"Not to take care of me. I can do that myself. I'm paying you for backup."

"Ah, yes. Backup." His dark eyes were twinkling again. "A lot of things can come under that heading, can't they?"

"Not the kind of things you're thinking about." She hitched up her jeans and stomped away from him.

"And how would you know what I'm thinking about, Mrs. O'Grady?"

Hands on her hips, she whirled back around and faced him. "Because you're a scoundrel, Mr. McGill."

"And we've already proven that you're no lady. That makes us quite a team."

"That makes us nothing. We're merely two people doing business who had the misfortune to be stranded together in the desert."

"We'll see." He rose from his seat on a rock and brushed off his jeans. "Are you going with me to look for a place to sleep, or do you plan to stand on that rock and pose for the rest of the evening?"

"I'm not posing."

"Yes, you are. And you do it so well." He stalked her and caught her by the arms. Her eyes went wide. "Don't worry. I'm not going to kiss you again."

"I'm not worried about that. I'm a married woman."

He grinned. "I don't need to be reminded. Do you?"

"You're positively the most arrogant, insufferable man I've ever met. For two cents I'd leave you stranded in the desert."

"Then how would you find your husband?" He tucked her hand through his arm and walked her toward a flat-topped mesa. "I suggest we seek higher ground. I wouldn't want to be asleep on the desert floor if a flash flood came."

"Being carried away by a flash flood might be preferable to sleeping with you."

He grinned. "Are you saying that I sweep you off your feet, Mrs. O'Grady?"

"I'm saying that you are one of nature's disasters. I'm surprised there aren't warning systems to protect people from you."

Chuckling, he led her upward. He knew they had reached higher ground when he heard the whistle of wings. A dark shadow passed over them, and they saw the raven, as black and mysterious as night, returning to his nest in a shallow hole in the canyon wall.

All around them the red and gray sandstones glowed in the intense setting sun. Distant mounains, ancient and wizened and wrinkled, cast shadows over the land. It was a sight so awesomely beautiful, they held their breaths. Nothing marred the silence except the piercing call of a canyon wren.

Suddenly the sun dropped from the sky. The Valley of Fire changed from a vibrant palette of reds and grays to a secret place shrouded in purple. With the sun went the heat. The landscape became cold and forbidding and hostile. Rustlings in the scrubby growth heralded the stirrings of nocturnal creatures.

"It seems we've reached our shelter not a moment too soon," Martha Ann said.

"My timing's always perfect."

"A pity your manners didn't match."

"Sweetheart, as much as I love these sparring matches with you, I suggest we gather enough twigs and branches to make a fire. We're liable to need it before the night is over."

They spent the next twenty minutes gathering brush for a fire. Some heat was still trapped in the rocks, so they set the branches aside for later use. Then, seated in the lee of an overhanging boulder, they assessed their supplies.

They had escaped the burning plane with almost nothing except the clothes on their backs. Rick's billfold and pipe and lighter were in his pockets, but Martha Ann had left her purse behind in the plane. Ditto their suitcases.

Rick held his lighter aloft. "This is it, kiddo. All that stands between us and the cold." He flicked the lighter, and it flared briefly in the darkness. Then he shoved it back into his pocket. "Of course, we have each other. Body heat."

"Don't look so smug. I don't intend to need your body heat. I have a sweater." Martha Ann drew her cotton sweater closer around her shoulders. Already

the desert air was turning cooler. The boulde
would furnish some protection from the wind tha
would swoop across the mesa unhampered, bu
it would be scant protection from the chill that woul
settle on the desert as the rocks lost their warmth. He
sweater would help but not much.

Both of them knew that.

They stared into space and contemplated the nigh
ahead. It would be dangerous all right. Nights in th
desert always were. But the greatest danger woul
not come from the chill nor the desert's creatures
The greatest danger would come from the chemistr
that sizzled between them. What they had to fea
most was themselves. The boulder they had choser
for shelter was covered with petroglyphs. Martha
Ann held the night at bay by telling one of the
Indian legends.

"Did you notice the drawing on that rock abov
your head?"

Rick snapped his lighter open and held it aloft. "I
looks like a beetle."

"That's Ko-Kapelli, the Flute Player. For the An
cient Ones who once lived here, he was the voice o
the Father Creator. His melodies of remembranc
kept the Ancient Ones from complacency. His son,
was a challenge to explore new lands, dream nev
dreams, build new societies. Often at night on th
desert, his song can still be heard."

"Have you ever heard him?"

"Yes. Many times."

"What is his song like?"

"Sometimes it's serene, like the soft sighing o
wind across the desert. Other times it's bold anc
brash, a harsh thundering that shakes the moun
tains, telling of Ko-Kapelli's rage."

"You speak with great authority about the Indians."

The history teacher in her was showing, and Rick was clever enough to see it. She hastened to make amends.

"It must be the Indian in me."

"You have Indian blood?"

"Doesn't everybody?" Her bloodlines were as pure as Irish linen. She figured her Irish ancestors were rolling in their graves. A few of the more irate ones might even take up haunting her small cottage in Fulton. It was another price she'd have to pay for deceit.

"Not me. I'm as Scottish as bagpipes."

Relieved that he hadn't pressed about her ancestors and her background, she leaned against the rock and pulled her sweater closer around her neck.

"Cold?"

She wasn't about to say yes, because she guessed that at the slightest hint from her that she was cold he'd pull her into his arms, bragging about his gallantry. Steeling herself against the creeping chill, she deliberately unbuttoned her sweater and fanned herself.

"Goodness no. I guess all that walking has warmed me up."

He didn't bother to hide his amusement. His big boom of laughter startled a raven into flight. In one swift move, he tossed a few sticks together and sat down so close, his thigh was brushing against hers.

"What are you doing?" she asked.

"Building a fire."

"A fire?"

He chuckled again. "Yes. What did you think I meant to do."

"Build a fire, of course." She scooted away so they were no longer touching. "I was thinking of conserving firewood, myself."

"We have enough to last a while." He flipped his lighter open and held it to the branches. They caught in a small blaze. "Just in case you get cold." He winked at her.

The wink nearly did her in. She loved being on the desert at night, and had often camped in this very valley during her teenage years. Having a companion had always doubled the fun. She and her friends used to sit around a campfire and swap Indian legends and ghost stories until the wee hours of the morning.

But Rick McGill was no teenager, and he certainly didn't have swapping ghost stories on his mind. That bold wink had told her all she needed to know. There was only one way to resist the temptation of that knowing wink.

She yawned and stretched. "I think I'll turn in. I've had a hard day." She turned her back to him and stretched out on the rocks, using her arms for a pillow.

"You can use my shoulder if you like."

"No thank you."

"Let me know if you change your mind."

"I'm very comfortable."

Rick wasn't ready for bed. The day had been long and traumatic, and he was still tightly wound up. He leaned against the rocks and gazed out across the Valley of Fire. It was hauntingly beautiful at night, shrouded in purple shadows and lit with random patches of light from the low-hanging moon.

He swung his gaze to Martha Ann. Her breathing had become regular. She was all tuckered out from her long day of pretending. He smiled as he remembered how she'd flown across the country, worrying her rosary, all the while pretending she wasn't afraid. After the crash she'd taken the Valley of Fire like

Patton invading Sicily, still pretending to be a pampered rich wife. And now she was curled on the rocks with her back to him, pretending that she was comfortable.

He drew the line at some things. Cold was one of them. Discomfort was another.

"Move over, baby. Here comes your Bogey." Grinning, he lay down beside her and pulled her into his arms spoon fashion. Body heat. He loved it.

"There now. Isn't that better?"

She snuggled closer to him and sighed. He grinned as he thought how mortified she'd be if she knew what she was doing.

She was as soft and cuddly as a golden retriever puppy. As he fitted himself comfortably against her sleeping form, his passion began to rise. He'd expected that. What he hadn't expected was tenderness. A great swell of protective feeling rose up in him. He felt a need to care for the woman in his arms, to protect her from the scurrying creatures of the desert, the cold wind that bore down on them, the unknown forces of the night. Such a feeling was new to him. And he was far too tired to wonder what it meant.

Closing his eyes, he fell asleep.

Ko-Kapelli's song whispered across the mesa, a soft melody as compelling as a lover's kiss.

Martha Ann moaned in her sleep and pressed closer to the warmth at her back. In his groggy state, Rick tightened his hold. Like homing pigeons, his hands sought the warmth of her breasts.

Ko-Kapelli's song became mischievous. It rippled over the mesa, bringing with it the chilly winds.

Martha Ann turned. Rick threw his leg over her hips. She pressed her open mouth against the warm skin at the collar of his shirt. Unconsciously his hands pulled her shirt out of its waistband and spread across her satiny back.

Ko-Kapelli laughed with glee. He howled and danced and swirled over the Valley of Fire, taking with him any bit of warmth remaining in the desert rocks.

Martha Ann and Rick, sleeping together on the mesa top, cuddled as close as lovers, receiving heat and comfort from each other.

In the early hours of dawn, Ko-Kapelli stole away, taking the cold with him.

Still half-asleep, Martha Ann stirred and attempted to stretch. She found herself held tight against the solid body of Rick McGill. She opened first one eye, then the other. Her mouth was pressed intimately against his neck; his leg was flung brazenly over her hips, and his hands were underneath her shirt. She knew she should have been outraged, but the simple fact was, she liked it.

She sighed. Wasn't that just like a Riley woman? She couldn't even get through one night without tumbling straight into the arms of this wife-chasing rake.

The real trick would be to make sure that it didn't happen again. She figured she could act rage as well as she could act rich

Drawing back as far as she could, she punched him in the ribs. "Let go of me."

"What the—" Rick's eyes flew open. Martha Ann's face was two inches from his nose, and she had murder in her eyes. He grinned. "Good morning, sweetheart. Sleep well?"

"Get your hands out from under my shirt."

"What a shame. That's such a nice place for my hands to be—even if I didn't know they were there."

"In a pig's eye, you didn't."

"Scout's honor." His hands were still under her shirt, and her skin felt so good, he saw no reason to resist a quick caress or two. So he didn't.

Martha Ann shivered, and it wasn't from the cold. "Will you stop that?"

He grinned. "You liked it, didn't you, Mrs. O'Grady."

"I did not. Remove your hands."

"Since I'm such a gentleman . . ." he paused, grinning at her, ". . . I'm bound to oblige." He took his time, dragging his fingertips over her back just so he could feel her shiver again. Chuckling, he tucked her shirt back into her waistband and patted her bottom. "There. Is that what you wanted, sweetheart?"

She'd gotten what she'd asked for and a lot more to boot. Darn his wicked hide, Rick McGill sure could charm a woman.

"It will be, as soon as you move your leg."

"Such a pity. I thought we were a great fit." He pressed his leg intimately against her hip before releasing his hold.

She scooted quickly away from him and stood up. The morning chill almost took her breath away.

Rick stood up and stretched. "Aren't you going to thank me?"

"Thank you?"

"I kept you from freezing to death last night."

"Nobody freezes to death in the middle of the desert in the summertime."

"I thought it best not to take chances."

"What you did was take advantage. And with a married woman."

"Tsk. Tsk." He made the small sound of remorse, but he didn't look the least bit remorseful. As a matter of fact, she thought he looked as pleased with himself as a naughty boy who had put a frog in the teacher's desk.

Since she couldn't fill him with regret, she decided to fill him with fear.

"It's a darned good thing Lucky didn't see you."

"You think he's out here in the desert? I thought he came to gamble."

"He did. He also likes to sightsee."

"At five o'clock in the morning?"

"You never know about him. He could turn up anywhere."

"I'm shuddering in my boots." He wasn't, of course. He was laughing.

Martha Ann tried one last play. "He has a terrible temper. You can just look at that picture of him I gave you in Dallas and tell." It was another lie, but she'd told too many to back down now. Her brother-in-law was a gambler and a wanderer, but he had the temperament of a sweet and people-pleasing cocker spaniel.

"I think I can outrun him. I ran track in college."

Rick McGill was a perfect scoundrel through and through. It was obvious to Martha Ann that she'd have nothing to depend on except her own strength of character to resist him. With her track record, that was like going up against a grizzly bear with a peashooter.

She dusted off her pants, raked her hand through her tumbled hair, and straightened her sweater. "I can tell you one thing, Rick McGill. This won't happen again."

"Martha Ann, there will always be a next time for people like us."

Four

In the early morning light, they left the Valley of Fire. After drinking their fill of water and filling their pockets with the beans of the catclaw acacia, they headed west toward Las Vegas. The distant mountains still wore their nightcaps of fog, and the red desert was just beginning to awaken. A family of prairie dogs, coming out of their burrows for breakfast, scolded the disheveled travelers as they passed through the valley.

Martha Ann and Rick ordinarily would have stopped to watch the chattering, lively little creatures, but they had miles to go before the sun turned the desert into an oven.

"Do you recall any ranches between here and Las Vegas, Martha Ann?"

"I remember two, but that was a long time ago. There is no way of knowing what's out there now."

"Don't worry. We're young and healthy. We can walk the entire fifty miles if we have to."

She thought it was nice to have a man who didn't make a bad situation worse by complaining. She smiled at him. "You're not such a bad guy, Rick McGill."

"You're not so bad yourself, Martha Ann O'Grady." He reached out and touched her cheek. "You have dust on your cheek."

"So do you." Impulsively, she brushed her hand across his cheek. She realized too late that was not at all the kind of thing Mrs. Lucky O'Grady should be doing. Under the guise of dusting herself off, she pulled back from him. "We must look like a couple of hobos."

"Make that hungry hobos. I keep thinking of a big juicy steak and fluffy biscuits and a mountain of scrambled eggs."

"It's cruel to mention food to a starving woman."

"I don't mean to be cruel, sweetheart. Just keeping the vision before you." He took her elbow. "Let's press on."

As they began their descent down a rocky incline, Martha Ann spotted the ribbon of paved road.

"Rick, look."

"By george, we're in luck."

They hurried toward the highway.

"Maybe a car will come along," Martha Ann said. "Maybe we'll get lucky."

They didn't.

Three hours later they were still walking. Although they had followed the winding path of the road, not a single car had darkened the horizon. Just when they were getting ready to take another break, they spotted a ramshackle fence. Their sagging spirits lifted like a bat-wing kite on a windy day.

"A ranch," Rick said.

"It's bound to be."

They joined hands and followed the fence, their faces shining with sweat and joy.

Clyde Running Bear was out beside his barn trying to decipher the mysteries of his ancient tractor. He knew nothing about repairing his wonderful machine, but that didn't keep him from trying. Putting down his wrench, he wiped his greasy hands across his greasy face and looked toward the horizon. He blinked and looked again.

"Velma!" He sprinted across his fine yard toward his grand house, scaring two chickens who were scratching in the dirt for worms. "Velma, honey! Shake a leg. We've got company."

The screen door flew open, and his wife appeared. She wore the sexy bright pink leotard that he loved so well. He stopped in silent appreciation of her beauty.

She wiggled her hips and winked. "What did you say about company, Clyde?"

"Are you trying to entice me, woman?"

"Always have and always will." The screen door slammed shut behind her, and she shimmied across the porch. "Do I look all right?"

"Honey, if we didn't have company coming, I'd show you just how all right you look."

"You Paiute devil, you."

Any other day he'd have let matters take care of themselves while he took care of his warm and willing bundle of beauty, but he had company coming. He pointed into the distance. "Look, there's two of them."

Velma shaded her eyes. "It looks like a couple of lovers."

"How can you tell?"

"I just know these things, Clyde." She descended the front porch steps, being careful to miss the broken fourth board. "How do you suppose they found us way out here, Clyde?"

"I guess the Lord sent 'em, Velma. He knows how lonesome you get for somebody besides me to talk to."

She reached up and patted the curls on her shiny blond wig. "Come on in," she yelled. "The gate's unlocked."

Rick and Martha Ann came through the gate. Six chickens watched them with malevolent eyes, and a fat, lazy dog merely yawned and went back to sleep beside the broken-down front proch. The ranch they had found wasn't exactly South Fork, Rick thought, but at least the owners would have water and a telephone. Keeping a tight and protective hold on Martha Ann's hand, he led her up the dusty path toward the waiting couple. The man was squat and square. His high-cheeked, pockmarked face was covered with grease, and two black braids hung onto the bib of his overalls. The woman beside him was tall and full-figured without being fat. Stage makeup covered a face that had probably once been pretty, and shiny sequins decorated her bright outfit.

"Hello," he said. "I'm Rick McGill, and this is my companion Martha Ann O'Grady."

Clyde stuck out his hand, then remembered it was greasy. He pulled it back, wiped it on his overalls, and offered it again. "Welcome to our house."

"We don't get much company," Velma said. "What brings you two out this way?"

"My private plane crashed in the Valley of Fire." Rick was dying of thirst and eager to get to a phone, but he supposed he'd be curious, too, if a couple of dusty strangers had turned up on his doorstep.

"You fly? I've always wanted to talk to somebody who could fly one of those things."

"Where are your manners, Clyde? These folks look hot and thirsty. Go out to the pump and get a bucket of fresh water." She took Martha Ann's hand and led her up the steps. "Come on in, you two. Land, how far did you have to walk? It's ten miles or more to the Valley. It must have been hotter than the devil's breath out there." She picked up a dingy cloth and wiped at the jelly stains on the back of two kitchen chairs. "Sit down. Clyde will be back with that water in a little while."

"Thank you." Martha Ann smiled at her hostess. "Water sounds wonderful."

"It certainly does." Rick rubbed Martha Ann's palm in a gesture of reassurance. The strain they'd been under since the previous day didn't show. She was sitting serenely in the jelly-stained chair as if she were planning to dine at the Ritz. She had class; there was no doubt about it. He relaxed a little. Their situation could have been worse.

"You two traveling together?" Velma noticed they were still holding hands. That pleased her. There was nothing she loved more than romance.

"Yes." Rick saw no reason to go into the whole story.

Martha Ann saw the gleam in Velma's eye and hastened to set her straight. "It's merely business. I've hired him to take me into Las Vegas."

They weren't fooling Velma. She was planning to pursue the subject a while longer, but Clyde came through the door with a bucket of water. She went to the cabinet and searched out two glasses that matched; then she filled them and set them before her guests.

"So, you two are going to Las Vegas?" She winked at Clyde.

"Las Vegas? That's where I met Velma. She was the prettiest thing out there. A dancer. Had legs so long, I swear she could kick the stars." He grinned at his wife.

Rick could tell that his host and hostess were enjoying themselves, but he was anxious to make arrangements for himself and Martha Ann. "That sounds like fun, Mister . . ." He waited for his host to supply his last name.

"Running Bear. I'm fifth generation Paiute."

"Mister Running Bear."

"Call me Clyde."

"Clyde, I wonder if I can use your phone?"

Clyde slapped his knee and chucked. "Did you hear that, Velma? He wants to use the phone."

Velma hooted with such full-bodied laughter, her false curls bounced up and down.

Rick didn't find his request funny, and he had a feeling that what he was going to hear next wouldn't make him laugh either.

"Clyde calls a phone the devil's own contraption."

"Not good for a thing except to tear a man's nerves to pieces. All that racket going on when a man's trying to eat or sleep or love his woman. I wouldn't have one of the things, myself."

"The noise is a consideration, of course." It took Rick's last bit of effort to be polite. He thought that one more piece of bad news would make him cuss, and he'd given up cussing fifteen years ago as a useless waste of time and breath. But he didn't want to hurt Clyde's feelings. Furthermore, there was Martha Ann to consider. He'd always prided himself on knowing how to take good care of a woman. So far he'd done a lousy job of it with her. It galled him that he had failed to get her to Las Vegas without mishap. The least he could do now was to stay calm and in control.

He bought time to put things back into perspective by drinking his water and studying his surroundings. The room looked as if it had been furnished by a garage sale addict. Three rusty bread boxes lined the counter. Beside them were two toasters, four spice racks, two automatic coffee makers, two sugar bowls, and three cracked teapots. Two clocks on the wall told the time, one a yellow tin rooster with a rusted red comb and glow-in-the-dark eyes, and the other a green plastic frog whose pink tongue flicked in and out on the quarter hour. It was nine-fifteen, and the tongue was moving in and out, mocking him.

It seemed that Mr. and Mrs. Clyde Running Bear had two of everything except a telephone.

Martha Ann smiled at him as if to say, "I can handle it." Rick patted her hand as if to say, "We'll make it."

"Does your neighbor have a phone?" Rick asked.

Clyde laughed again. "He's got one, but he's twenty miles away."

"I wonder if you could drive us. I'd pay you, of course."

"I'll be glad to . . . as soon as my truck's fixed."

Rick wondered if he was paying for all his past sins and indiscretions. "How long will that be?"

"Could be two days or could be two weeks. Ralph picked it up last week and said it would be ready soon. But time doesn't mean a thing to him."

"Now don't you two worry," Velma said. "We've got plenty of room, and we'll be pleased to have company."

"Absolutely. Why, when Ralph brings back my truck, I'll take you into Las Vegas myself."

"Can I go too, Clyde?"

"That's what I had in mind all along, honey. The trip will do you good. It'll be just like a picnic, the four of us in that truck. We'll set up chairs in the back end."

Throughout this exchange, Rick and Martha Ann had been watching each other. Their expressions had run the gamut from disbelief to resignation to wry humor.

"Thank you for that gracious invitation," Martha Ann said.

"We accept," Rick added.

"I'll bet you two are starving to death." Velma jumped up and began to bustle around the kitchen. In short order she had set two plates of warmed over refried beans in front of her guests. "You two eat hearty. Clyde and I have plans to make."

Their hosts went out the front door.

Rick looked at the beans on his plate and thought of the beans still in his pockets. Martha Ann began to chuckle.

"Are you thinking what I'm thinking?" he asked.

"Yes." She picked up her fork and took a mouthful. "But I never question a gift horse."

"I think that's 'look a gift horse in the mouth.' "

"Whatever." She took another forkful. "You know, you've handled yourself very well in this situation. I like a man with a sense of humor. I might even get to like you in spite of your notorious wife-chasing ways."

"You're a champ yourself, Mrs. Lucky O'Grady. If I'm not careful, I'm going to let liking you get in the way of my plans."

The remark about his plans was loaded. Martha Ann decided to ignore it. "I always try to count my blessings. We're not in such bad shape after all. Clyde and Velma are sweet, and a soft bed tonight will be wonderful."

"It certainly will." He grinned.

"Soft *separate* beds."

"Sweetheart, the distance between two beds is very short."

"You're going to find out just how impossible that journey is."

"Good. Easy victories bore me."

"I can promise you one thing, Rick McGill: You won't be bored."

"I can hardly wait."

After they had eaten their beans, Rick went outside with Clyde to give him advice on fixing the magnificent but ailing Ford tractor, and Martha Ann stayed behind with Velma.

Even though the women were using a dishpan and water heated on the stove, they made quick work of the dirty dishes.

"It's just wonderful to have somebody to talk to." Velma dried her hands on the dishtowel. "Clyde's a love, of course, but he grew up out here in the middle of the desert with nothing but jackrabbits. Me . . . I'm a city girl. I like bright lights and crowds of people. Say, I'll bet you lost everything you had in that plane crash."

"All I have are the clothes on my back." Martha Ann smiled. "But I'm still in one piece. That's what counts."

"Don't you worry about a thing. You're tall enough to wear my things. I've got a little more hip than you now, but in my day I was just as slim and pretty as you are." She took Martha Ann's hand and led her into a bedroom that looked like something straight out of *The Arabian Nights*. Gossamer curtains and gold tassels draped the walls and the beds. Dozens of candles in brass candlesticks decorated the two bedside tables and the top of the dresser. It was a fantasy room made for love.

"You like it?"

"I think it's a wonderful room." Martha Ann *did* think it was wonderful. She'd never let convention dictate her own tastes and life-style, and it was obvious that neither did Velma. She'd found a soul mate. "I really do, Velma."

"Great. Then you'll love the clothes I'm going to lend you." Velma reached into her closet and pulled out a hot pink harem suit. The legs were slit at the sides and the minuscule top was decorated with rhinestones. "One of my old costumes. I think it will fit."

Martha Ann took the elaborate stage costume. "Are you sure, Velma? It's much too pretty to wear around the house."

"Shoot. I believe in gilding the lily." She reached back into her closet and came out with a nightgown that would have caused legions of angels to fall from grace. "Here, you can wear this tonight . . . unless you prefer sleeping in the nude." She winked.

Martha Ann looked at the gown. It was so sheer and sexy she'd feel naughty wearing it even in the privacy of her own bedroom. "Are you sure about this, Velma? I don't want to impose."

"All that stuff's too little for me now. You wear it while you're here. Enjoy life. That's what I say."

"Thanks, Velma. And now if you could show me the bathroom, I'd love to take a bath."

"I guess you forgot; we don't have running water. But we've got the finest bathtub in the world—the creek."

"What about privacy?"

Velma laughed. "You don't have to worry about being seen. The creek's a long way from the house, and there's nothing for miles around except a few jackrabbits and some straggly old cows and a sidewinder or two. You'll have as much privacy as you would in the finest hotel—and you'll be just as pampered." She delved into her dresser drawers and came out with a large plastic bottle. Seduction, the label said. "Bubble bath," Velma said. "Guaranteed to do the trick."

The only trick Martha Ann wanted to do was get rid of the dirt on her and on her clothes. She took the bubble bath, a towel, and the borrowed harem suit, then Velma showed her the way to the creek.

It was a secluded spot, far enough away from the house to guarantee privacy and shielded by a thick growth of bushes and several large cottonwood trees.

After Velma had gone, Martha Ann stripped off her dirty clothes and washed them in the creek. Then she spread them on stones to dry.

The sun felt so good that she stood for a moment, trying to decide whether to take a bath or a nap. She chose to take a bath. She followed the winding creek downstream to a spot where the water pooled into a quiet lagoon. Velma had been right. It was the finest bathtub in the world. The water was deep blue and serene, dappled with the sunlight that filtered through the branches of overhanging trees.

Clutching her bottle of bubble bath, Martha Ann waded in. The shaded water was chilly, and she shivered. She moved slowly toward deeper water, taking time to get used to the temperature. When she was waist-deep, she plunged her head under and came up dripping. Feeling refreshed and reckless, she dumped the bubble bath into the creek and stirred the water with her hands to create a foam. Bubbles swirled around her.

She scooped a handful of bubbles up with one hand and tossed the bottle over her head with the other.

Rick McGill came out of the bushes just in time to catch the flying bottle. It landed with a plop in his outstretched hand. He had thought the sounds he'd heard coming from the creek were being made by an old cow, but he was wrong. They were made by Martha Ann Riley. She was waist-deep in the water, her hair slicked back from her head, and her back shiny with sunshine and bubbles. For a moment he thought he'd died and been transported to Glory Land. He'd hoped for a bath and had gotten a vision instead. Fate was smiling on him after all.

"How's the water, sweetheart?"

Martha Ann's back stiffened and shivers went up her spine. Good grief, she thought. Here she was without her clothes, and Rick McGill had her trapped. It was just like him to pull such a stunt. And just when she was beginning to trust him.

She ducked out of sight under the water and tried to think what to do.

"No need to be modest, sweetheart. I've seen naked women before."

His wicked chuckle echoed across the water. Martha Ann had held her breath so long, she was beginning to get light-headed. She'd have to do something soon. It would serve him right if she just marched up the bank buck naked and gave him a piece of her mind.

"If you don't come on out, I'll have to come in and get you."

He would, too, she thought. Still holding her breath, she knee-walked toward deeper water. When she judged that she was deep enough, she turned around and stood up. She'd miscalculated by half an inch. The twinkle in his eye told her that he thought he was the cause of all that puckering.

She quickly stepped backward into water deep enough to cover the tops of her breasts. "Don't look so smug. The water's cold."

"My, my. How the lady does protest." He stood there with a self-satisfied smirk on his face, looking as if he could see straight under the water, and enjoying every bit of what he saw.

"You can turn around and leave, Rick McGill. I don't plan to provide entertainment."

"I came for a bath. The entertainment is an added attraction."

He tossed the plastic bottle to the ground and began to unbutton his shirt.

"What do you think you're doing?"

"Undressing. I always bathe in the nude."

"Don't you dare set foot in this water."

He laughed. "I think the creek's big enough for two."

She watched with fascination as he stripped off his shirt and flung it to the ground. His chest looked so good, it could set saints to sinning. She wished she had her rosary.

Rick sat down on the ground and took off his shoes. He hadn't expected to encounter Martha Ann at the creek, but that didn't change his plans one bit. He was hot and tired, and he was going to have his bath. Having her there only added a little spice to the afternoon.

He stood up and unbuckled his belt.

"Don't you dare take off your pants."

"You don't expect me to bathe with my pants on, now do you?" Grinning, he hooked his thumbs in the waistband of his jeans and began to inch them down over his hips.

Until he started pulling off his pants, Martha Ann had thought she could win this contest of wills. Now, she began to wonder. She decided to change her tactics.

"If you think you're going to entice me by showing me the merchandise, Rick McGill, you'd better know this: I'm not interested."

The pants kept moving downward. "If you don't want to see the merchandise, sweetheart, you'd better turn around."

She whirled around so fast her feet slipped out from under her. She came up sputtering, but this time with her back toward him.

"You are the cockiest . . ."

"Not at the moment, my dear."

". . . most arrogant, bullheaded, aggravating, unscrupulous man I've ever had the misfortune to meet." Behind her she could hear him undressing. He was making a big to-do of it, primarily to irritate her, she guessed. She crossed her arms over her chest and continued her tirade.

"If that's not just like you to plan this ravishment in the creek . . ."

"Ravishment in the creek." He hooted with laughter. Martha Ann Riley, a.k.a. Mrs. Lucky O'Grady, might not have planned to provide entertainment, but she was certainly doing a super job of it. Ravishment in the creek. He chuckled again. It sounded like the name of a low-budget movie.

He tossed his pants on the ground and waded into the creek. "My dear, I prefer my women sweet, and at the moment you are about as sweet as a crock of pickles left too long in the brine."

A crock of pickles. That did it!

"If you take one step more, you're a dead man."

"What I am right now is a dirty man . . ."

"I'll say . . ."

". . . and I intend to wash."

He made so much racket in the water, he sounded like two Brahman bulls. Naturally he would, she fumed. He wanted her to know he was washing that fabulous chest of his. If it hadn't been for his chest, she might have stayed in the creek and fought it out with him. But there was that chest, as tan as a copper penny and looking better than strawberry ice cream on a hot day. Goodness gracious. She'd never be able to resist it if she stayed.

"Since you insist on ruining my bath, I'm leaving."

He chuckled. "So soon, sweetheart? The fun's just getting started."

"Not with me, it's not." She started toward the creek bank, then stopped to warn him. "And don't you dare look."

"I wouldn't dream of it, being the gentleman I am."

He kept his word. She waded all the way to the bank while his back was turned. Quickly she snatched up her towel and draped it around herself. It covered the essentials.

She was reaching for her shoes when he turned around.

"You look fetching in that towel."

She decided to have one last word.

"If you think not watching me leave the water has

redeemed you, you're sadly mistaken. Nothing you can do, no apology you can ever make will cleanse your black-hearted, wife-chasing soul."

She spun around, picked up the harem suit, and was halfway up the bank before he spoke.

"I never make apologies."

She'd just have to let him have the last word, she decided. If she turned back around she'd see his chest. And if she saw his chest one more time, there was no telling what kind of fool she'd make of herself.

She'd have to content herself with stomping. It was what she'd always done when Evelyn had gotten the best of her.

As she stomped off, she heard him laughing.

Velma and Clyde heard it all. They were hiding in the thick bushes beside the creek, checking on the progress of their plan.

"Good Lord, Velma," Clyde whispered, "do you think I ought to peek through there and see what's going on? She sounds mad enough to kill him."

"I draw the line at spying, Clyde."

Velma and Clyde prided themselves on being experts in love. Weddings didn't matter to them; they'd never bothered with one themselves. What they understood was passion. And they'd seen it in Rick and Martha Ann. Their job, as they saw it, was to give that passion an opportunity. Maybe even an assist.

"Velma, do you think I should have waited till she finished her bath before I sent him down there to the creek?"

"Shoot. That wouldn't have worked. She might have had her clothes back on."

"Maybe I should have told him she'd be down there. Some men don't like surprises."

"I never knew a man who didn't like a surprise like that." Velma clutched his arm. "Shoot, Clyde. Listen to that. I think she's leaving."

He patted her hand. "Don't look so blue, Velma honey. I've got a plan."

Dinner that evening was straight out of a Marx Brothers movie. Velma and Clyde were sitting out on the front porch pretending they wanted to eat in the open air. It was one of the flimsiest excuses Martha Ann had ever heard for leaving her alone with Rick McGill. She decided that she was really getting her money's worth. She had wanted to have some excitement while finding her brother-in-law. Between Mr. and Mrs. Running Bear and Rick McGill, she was getting almost more than she bargained for. Almost but not quite. She was equal to anything.

Rick was leaning back in his chair across the kitchen table from her, relaxed and good-humored and looking as innocent as a little boy in his Sunday best on the front pew during church services. But she could feel the excitement, the tension in him. There was no telling what he would do or say next. The uncertainty thrilled her. She loved her profession, but teaching history was so predictable, so routine that she craved the glamour of the unknown.

Something was bound to happen. She could feel it.

"That's a remarkable costume you're wearing, Mrs. O'Grady."

Rick had used her formal title. That was a tip-off that he was up to something. Martha Ann shivered in anticipation.

"Thank you. It's Velma's."

"It's one of her stage costumes, isn't it?"

"I think so."

"When's the show?"

"I beg your pardon."

Rick pushed his plate aside, folded his hands behind his head, and tipped his straight chair back on two legs.

"Since you're dressed in that harem suit, I thought you might do the Dance of the Seven Veils for me."

"Sorry. I'm not a performer."

He chuckled. "That was quite a show you put on this afternoon . . ."

"That was no show."

". . . pretending to be outraged when I knew all along that you were having as much fun as I was."

She repressed her grin. That scamp had seen straight through her. Besides that, he was the most aggressive man she'd ever met. Nothing deterred him. She'd tried intimidation, direct orders, fear, rejection. Nothing worked with Rick McGill.

There was one last thing she could try. Cutting a small bite of tough steak, she set out to tame Rick McGill with boredom.

Her first ploy was not to initiate any conversation. She sat back in her chair and chewed as if her life depended on it.

Rick hadn't caught on yet.

"What did you do this afternoon?"

No reply. She merely shrugged her shoulders and attacked her soggy potatoes.

"Clyde and I spent the afternoon trying to repair his tractor." He paused, waiting. She said nothing. "He told me several Indian legends."

She couldn't treat him to complete silence. He'd think she was pouting, and she never pouted.

"That's nice," she said.

"Velma came out three times to see about us."

"That's nice."

"She brought cold lemonade."

"That's nice."

Suddenly Rick's chair banged to the floor. He strode around the table and lifted her from her chair.

"What the . . ."

"Just checking to see if you're still in there somewhere."

He turned her around and pulled her so close, her breath swooshed out. Taking one of her arms, he draped it around his shoulders.

"Now, Mrs. Lucky O'Grady, let's see how nice you think this is."

Without further ado, his mouth came down on hers.

"Mmft mmt." She struggled and protested for all of two seconds, and then the adventuress in her gave up to the scoundrel in him. She wrapped her other arm around his neck and pulled his head closer. "Mmmmm." She couldn't have kept that sound of satisfaction from escaping her lips if she'd wanted to. But she didn't want to. Acting the married woman was a totally ineffective defense against Rick McGill. She'd have to think of something else. But not now. Now she was going to enjoy this kiss.

She pressed so close, she could feel the heavy thudding of his heart. His lips were expert, but so were hers. Her ex-husband Marcus had taught her how to kiss, and she'd thought he was the world's all-time best kisser. Until now. Until Rick.

She opened herself to him, heart and soul. What they were doing suddenly stopped being technique and became magic. She couldn't explain what was happening. She couldn't describe it. She could only feel.

She soared again and gave herself up to the magic.

Rick was teaching her a lesson. That's what he kept telling himself. He was also having a mild flirtation. He kept telling himself that too. But then why was his heart beating so fast, it felt as if it would fly out of his chest, and why was his blood pounding in his ears?

He moved his hands over her torso. It was bare beneath the miniscule halter top. Other women just had soft skin. Why did hers feel like silk? Why couldn't he get enough of touching her?

When she pressed closer and moaned, his blood all left his brain. The need exploded in him with such force that he growled deep in his throat. But it was more than need, more than desire. It was something so indescribably beautiful that he couldn't begin to fathom it. He could only feel.

Bending her slightly backward, he delved into her mouth with his tongue. It was heaven. It was like flying through the skies at night with the stars so close, he could feel their heat on his face.

He moved his hands over her. The harem pants were obligingly slit in all the right places. Her legs were trim and tight and silken. By george, every inch of her skin was silk. He was dangerously close to being enchanted.

One last taste, one last dip into that heavenly mouth, one last touch—that's all he would allow himself. His mouth slanted over hers, and her response sent jolts of lightning through him. Maybe two, he decided. No more than three.

At last he knew there was no hope for him except to stop. He broke off the kiss and stared down at her long enough to give him time to catch his breath.

"Now, let's hear you say 'that's nice.' " He hadn't known voices really got gruff with passion until he heard his own. He was barely on the edge of control. He hoped she didn't notice.

Martha Ann took a shaky breath. "That's nice, but your technique could use some polishing."

"Perhaps we should try again."

"Sorry. I'm taken." She sat hastily back down in her chair. "You'll just have to find some sweet unattached young woman to teach you the finer points of kissing."

"What a pity. You kiss with such enthusiasm."

"I wasn't kissing."

"You weren't?" He went to the other side of the table and sat down, grinning. "What were you doing?"

"I was just exercising my mouth." She put down her fork and pursed her lips in a series of contortions. "See. It helps keep wrinkles from forming." She picked up her fork and ate a small bite of string beans, taking her time chewing. "A woman my age has to think of these things."

He laughed. "What else does a woman your age think of? You, in particular."

"Oh, lots of things. Music, theater, politics, education."

"Let's take music. Do you like jazz? Pop? Blues? Classical? Golden oldies?"

"All of them, especially golden oldies. Everything about the forties fascinates me."

Rick took a big bite of steak, thinking. He should have known. A woman who could kiss and who liked golden oldies to boot. Of course, she was scared to death of flying, which was a great passion of his, but two out of three wasn't bad.

"I suppose you're a Republican?"

"Dyed-in-the-wool Democrat."

"Then you hate taxes but love giveaway programs."

"I think that excellence in anything has its price. If that price is higher taxes, then I'm willing to pay my share. Especially for education."

Clyde and Velma walked into the room in time to hear the political discussion. Their hopes fell. They would have been happy if Rick and Martha Ann had been discussing the weather or Las Vegas or food or even snake killing—anything except politics. They exchanged a glance that said their guests definitely needed rescuing.

Velma slid into a chair beside Martha Ann, and Clyde sat down across the table beside Rick.

Velma patted Martha Ann's arm. "How about this girl in my costume? Is she sensational or what?"

Rick grinned. "It's nice."

Martha Ann nearly choked on her potatoes.

Velma tried again. "You should have heard Clyde bragging on Rick. Why, he said that man has more knowledge of machines in his little finger than Ralph has in his whole head." She paused dramatically and turned to Martha Ann, waiting for a comment.

"That's nice." Martha Ann gave Rick a mischievous grin.

"Well . . ." Velma kicked Clyde under the table.

"Uh . . . there's a lovely moon out tonight."

Velma beamed. "It sure is. Just right for a walk in the moonlight."

"You two go and have a great time," Martha Ann said. "Rick and I will clean up the kitchen."

Velma kicked under the table again, missing Clyde and nailing Rick in the shin. He grunted.

"The high point of Clyde's day is helping me with the dinner dishes." Velma's lethal foot struck again.

"Owwww . . . Oh, o, that's right." Clyde pushed back his chair and hobbled around the table. "You two go on and enjoy the moon. Velma and I will wash up."

"That's a wonderful idea," Rick said. "I've been sitting here trying to get up enough courage to ask Martha Ann for a walk in the moonlight."

Martha Ann smothered her derisive hoot with her hand. Rick McGill had enough courage to slay an invasion of hostile Martians and still have enough left over to share with the entire U.S. Army.

"What a *nice* idea." She stood up. "It will be such a *nice* walk."

Rick came around the table, took her elbow, and escorted her toward the door. Leaning down, he whispered, "It had better not be."

Five

The minute they were out the door, Martha Ann sat down on the front porch steps, being careful to choose a board that was not rickety.

"I'm not going a step. I'm tired and my feet hurt and I don't want to be off in the dark with you."

"You suspect me of impure motives?" Rick propped one foot on the step beside her and leaned his elbow on his knee. "I'm crushed."

"You look about as crushed as an elephant in an orange juice press."

"At least you've decided not to be nice."

"I may never be nice again as long as I live. I was beginning to bore myself."

Rick laughed. It was amazing to him how often he laughed with Martha Ann. Most women he knew took themselves and life too seriously. Not her, though. She just went zinging through life, doing whatever came naturally. She would wear well. Fifty years from now she'd be as much fun as she was today. Not that he'd be around her fifty years from now. He wasn't looking for a woman to grow old with. Not yet, anyhow. But still . . .

"Do you think we'll be here two weeks, Rick?"

"Don't worry about that. Even if Ralph doesn't get Clyde's truck repaired, I think I can have that tractor in running condition in another day or so. If necessary I can drive it to the nearest ranch and arrange transportation to Las Vegas."

"Good. I have to be back home in two weeks."

"You do?"

She remembered too late that she was supposed to be a wealthy woman without obligations.

"Society appointments . . . charity benefits and the like. Nothing I can't cancel though. But I am anxious to find my husband."

"I'd say you're a woman desperately in need of a husband."

"I wouldn't say 'desperately.' "

"No. But your kisses do."

"Why, you blackguard!" She left the steps and marched across the yard, her back stiff.

He caught up with her and took her arm. "Going for a walk? I think I'll go too."

"I don't know how you ever expect to find a wife . . ."

"I'm not looking."

". . . because you don't take anything seriously. One minute you're just as good as you can be, talking about your plans for getting us to a telephone, and the next you're so wicked, your own grandmother would disown you."

"I'm her favorite grandson."

He steered her toward the barn and the shade of a large cottonwood tree. Even though the sun had gone down it was still hot outside. Releasing her arm, he leaned against the tree trunk.

"Let's stop right here. I've done enough walking today to last me a lifetime."

"Then why did you act so eager to go on this walk?"

"I didn't want to hurt Velma's and Clyde's feelings. You know, of course, that they're trying as hard as they can to get the two of us together."

"You don't need any help. That bit at the creek this afternoon . . ."

". . . was all their doing. Clyde sent me down there. On purpose, I think."

"Good grief."

"Not that I'm complaining. I loved every minute of it."

So had she, but she wasn't going to tell him. She walked a few paces from him and picked up a slender cottonwood branch. Her mind replayed the day's event as she thrust the makeshift foil into the air. Somewhere between the night in the Valley of Fire and the encounter beside the creek, she'd lost sight of her primary purpose: Finding her sister's husband. She *had* to concentrate, she told herself. She had to learn to resist the charming rake beside her. She had to . . .

"Do you fence?"

She neatly parried an imaginary thrust and turned to him. "Yes."

He picked up a branch to match her own. "En garde."

His attack was expert and aggressive. Their wooden foils clashed in the darkness as they dueled. His strength was superior, but she was quick. She neatly parried a head cut and began her riposte.

"You're good, Mrs. O'Grady."

She scored a point to his chest. The wooden foil quivered there, and she smiled. "Lost your concentration, didn't you?"

"Only for a moment. It's those rhinestones that keep distracting me."

Martha Ann had forgotten about her costume. It was designed to reveal. And right now, with all that fencing activity, it was revealing more than any self-respecting Episcopalian would dare. To top it all off, her skin was gleaming with sweat and the reflected glow of rhinestones, and Rick McGill was appreciating every exposed inch of it.

"Are we still playing, Mrs. O'Grady?"

"Playing?"

He chuckled. "Fencing?"

"Of course." She leaped and lunged, but her own concentration had disappeared.

Rick scored a quick point. The tip of his wooden foil barely touched her chest, right between her cleavage. She stood, panting.

"I didn't hurt you, did I?"

"No." The makeshift foil still rested intimately on her breasts. She wished he would move it.

"You're sure? I get carried away with games, and we're not dressed for fencing."

The tip of his foil moved, circling slowly, intimately on her skin. She thought it was deliberate, but she couldn't be sure.

"I'm fine. Just a little hot."

"You're hot?" His smile was devilish. The foil moved again, this time tracing along the tops of her breasts.

She drew in a sharp breath. "It's the desert. I'd forgotten how hot it can be out here."

"Steamy." The tip of his foil nudged the thin material downward. She felt herself responding to the sensual play of his sword.

"Such heat can be downright scary." She was almost panting now.

"Even dangerous." His smile was slow and lazy. The limber foil skimmed underneath the rhinestones and found her nipple. Rick's foil teased her, played with her, excited her.

She was mesmerized. She couldn't have moved if she had wanted to. And she didn't want to. She was at the mercy of this wicked man and his sensual sword.

Rick was panting now. His breath came in harsh gasps. What had started as fun was turning into something else. He sensed that he could have an easy victory there under the cottonwood tree, but he wasn't ready for that yet. He wanted to enjoy the chase a while longer.

He gazed at Martha Ann. In the moonlight the beauty spot above her lips looked more fetching than ever. And her hair—it was so black and lush a man could disappear in it and never be found again. Raven's wing, velvet black, midnight dark. Some crazy fool poet in his soul was making him think in metaphors.

The tip of his foil faltered. Looking into her eyes, he slowly withdrew his sword. They didn't speak for a while but stood watching each other. Finally she closed her eyes and took a deep breath.

When she opened them, he had his sword pointed toward the ground.

"I don't want to finish this game," she said.

"Neither do I." He tossed the cottonwood branch aside and took her elbow. "Let's go back inside."

They didn't talk as they went back to the main house. After that intimate swordplay, there seemed nothing much to say.

The screen door popped behind them, and they walked into the brightly lit room. At one end the dishes were stacked in the sink, unwashed, and at the other end Velma and Clyde sat in two sagging easy chairs, Velma doing needlepoint and Clyde watching two TVs. The large color console set was tuned to a hell-fire-and-damnation evangelist, and the small black-and-white portable atop the color TV was tuned to a baseball game. Clyde was alternately cussing and saying amen, sometimes saying the amens when the Dodgers scored a run and cussing when he was supposed to be praying.

It was a sight to see. It was also a relief, for it served to break the spell of sensuality that had bound Rick and Martha Ann. They grinned at each other.

Velma looked up from her needlepoint. "You're back. Did you have a good walk?"

"The moon was lovely," Martha Ann said.

"The stars have never been brighter," Rick added.

Velma checked out their flushed faces. Her plan was working. Tonight would be the finishing touch. She grinned, pleased with herself.

"Clyde, they had a good time."

"Amen."

"Clyde!" His head jerked up, and he looked at his wife.

"You say something, Velma?"

"I said they had a *good* time."

"Well, now, that's just wonderful. Just *great*." He smiled at his guests for a while, and then smiled at Velma. He might not know much about tractors, but he did know about love. He'd known a walk in the moonlight would do the trick. Finally, remembering his manners, he jumped up and offered Martha Ann his chair. "Here. You take this comfortable seat."

"Thank you, but this one will be fine." She started toward a straight-backed kitchen chair, but Rick intercepted. He carried two chairs across the room to where Velma and Clyde were sitting. He and Martha Ann sat down side by side.

"Clyde, turn up that preacher. Can you two hear all right?"

"Great," Rick said.

"We'll watch something else if you want to," Clyde said. "There's not much on tonight though."

"I like games." Rick winked at Martha Ann. "Especially baseball," he said to Clyde.

For the next two hours they sat on the hard chairs watching the two television screens with Clyde and Velma. The best Rick could tell the Dodgers hit a homerun somewhere around Revelation, the Cardinals struck out in the middle of Ezekiel, and fourteen sinners got saved in the bottom of the sixth inning. It was an incredible evening.

When the two clocks struck ten, Velma and Clyde looked at each other and winked. Velma disappeared briefly, then came back and announced, "Bedtime."

"That sounds great," Martha Ann said. "It has been a very long day."

"For me too." Rick stood up and stretched. "A soft bed will feel great."

"You two follow me, and I'll show you to your room."

Room? Martha Ann thought. She looked at Rick, and he shrugged his shoulders as if to say, "Beats me."

The ranch house consisted of the front room, which served as kitchen, dining, and living area, and two small bedrooms separated by a tiny hall.

Velma opened a door and swept her arm grandly through the air. "Here it is. Just like mine." She grinned at them. "I believe in giving my guests all the comforts of home."

The bedroom was identical to the one Martha Ann had seen earlier. Exotic curtains were draped around the bed and over the walls, and scented candles were already lit and burning in every corner of the room.

Martha Ann felt her stomach tighten. One bedroom. She should have realized earlier how small the house was. She should have known it couldn't possibly have two guest bedrooms. She guessed she'd been too tired or too hot or too hungry to notice.

She swung her gaze to Rick. He was taking it all in stride. In fact, he was even smiling. Saints preserve her. What would she do?

Velma was watching her expectantly. She felt compelled to say something. "It's lovely, Velma. Thank you."

"I knew you'd like it . . . you two traveling together, and all." She began to back out of the room. "Well, you two have a good night's sleep."

The door clicked shut behind her. Clyde was waiting for her in the hall.

"How did it go, Velma? Did they like it?"

"The best I could tell they did. Are you sure everything's in place?"

"Right where it ought to be. I had to make a few substitutions though. It's an old recipe, and you can't find the ear of a bison anymore."

"What did you use?"

"Remember that old heifer that got sick on the range and died last week?"

"Yes."

"The buzzards hadn't gotten to the ears yet. I used one of them."

"I'm just dying to know how everything's going in there."

"We might be able to hear if we pressed our ears up against the wall."

"Clyde! I'm shocked at you. Some things are private matters." She smoothed her hands over her hips and patted her wig. "Let's go, honey. I believe in letting things take their natural course."

Clyde and Velma linked arms and went down the hall to their own bedroom, secure in the knowledge that love was taking its natural course—thanks to a little assistance from them.

Inside the guest bedroom Rick and Martha Ann were squared off on opposite sides of the bed.

"Quit looking so pleased," she said.

"Who? Me? I didn't plan this."

"But I'll bet you're perfectly willing to take advantage of the situation."

"It takes two, sweetheart."

Martha Ann ignored that comment. She glanced toward the hard floor. "I suppose one of us could make a pallet down there."

"I'll sleep on the floor, Mrs. O'Grady. You take the bed."

She chewed her lower lip. "It looks so uncomfortable down there."

"It's not my idea of a perfect place to sleep, but it will do."

She patted the mattress. "It seems a shame." She glanced at Rick, who was still standing on the other side of the bed. "After all, you did spend last night sleeping on the rocks."

"So did you."

"It's a big bed."

"It is."

"I suppose you could stay on your side."

"And you could stay on yours."

"We could even put a divider in the middle, a rolled up sheet or something."

"A Wall of Jericho."

She knew exactly what he was talking about, for she loved old movies. It had been a while since she'd seen Clark Gable in *It Happened One Night,* but she distinctly remembered the night the Walls of Jericho came tumbling down.

She lifted her chin. "We're both adults. We don't need a Wall of Jericho. We'll just agree to stay on opposite sides of the bed."

He grinned. "A gentleman's agreement."

"Precisely."

He hurried around the bed. She backed against the wall.

"I always seal my bargains, Mrs. O'Grady."

"I know."

Grinning, he stuck out his hand. "With a hand-shake. Remember?"

"Of course. I was just resting." She leaned against the wall a while longer and even threw in a big yawn for effect, then she took his hand.

The handshake was brief and firm and businesslike.

"Well, now. That's done. Since I'm a gentleman, I'll let you undress first."

"Undress?"

"You don't plan to sleep in your clothes, do you?"

"Of course not. Velma lent me a gown."

"I'll turn my back while you change."

He did. She changed into the gown, which was not much better than being naked, and slid quickly under the sheets.

"All finished," she said.

He turned back around. "How's the bed?"

"Comfortable." She pulled the covers up to her chin.

"Cold?" Rick began to unbutton his shirt.

"No. . . . Yes. That's the funny thing about these nights in the desert. You can be burning up one minute and freezing the next."

"I'm willing to warm you up." He peeled off the shirt and reached for his belt buckle.

"No!" She fanned the sheets. "Actually, I'm a little hot." He gave her a knowing grin. She decided to change the subject. "Did Clyde give you pajamas to sleep in?"

"I'm afraid not, pet. Anyway, I don't wear pajamas."

"You don't?"

"I sleep in the nude."

She suddenly wished she had put up a Wall of Jericho.

"But don't worry," Rick added. "Since I'm in bed with a married lady, I'll keep my shorts on."

"You had better."

"At least for a little while."

When he began to slide his pants down over his hips, she squeezed her eyes shut. She felt the gossamer curtains being drawn back, felt the mattress sag, and heard the bedsprings creak. There was a small swishing sound as Rick dropped the curtain and settled down into bed.

He stretched and yawned under the guise of getting comfortable, but she figured he was doing all that movement to get her attention. She kept her eyes shut, her legs pressed tightly together, and her hands straight down by her sides. It was as relaxing as being on the stretching rack during the Spanish Inquisition.

His foot touched hers. "Excuse me."

"Certainly." She jerked her foot away.

He rolled over in the bed. His hand brushed against her shoulder. She couldn't move away without falling off the bed, so she waited for him to move his hand. Goose bumps popped out on her arm, and she prayed to be rescued from her own feelings.

"Sorry." He was as slow as molasses in December moving his hand, and when he did, he dragged it down the whole length of her arm. She hoped he didn't feel her goose bumps.

He finally settled down on his side of the bed, not touching, and she tried to relax. It was impossible. Even the sound of his breathing bothered her. Not that it was unpleasant. On the contrary. She found it extremely pleasant, reassuring even.

She turned her back to him, hoping it would help. It didn't. Her hips hiked up the sheet between them so that she could feel his body heat. Oh, help, she thought. What was she to do? She tried counting sheep, but thoughts of Rick kept creeping into her mind, and she lost count at eight. Or was it nine?

He moved, and his leg brushed against hers. She decided to let it stay there. What was the harm?

The minutes dragged by. Martha Ann felt sweat trickle between her breasts. She had the choice of smothering to death or kicking down the sheet. Being practical, she kicked down the sheet.

"Are you hot?"

"Sorry, I didn't mean to wake you."

"I wasn't asleep."

"Neither was I." Bold as he was, he would probably take that admission as an invitation. Her mind groped for a distraction. She wasn't long in finding it. "Do you smell something funny?"

"It must be the candles."

"Good grief, the candles." She sat straight up in bed. Too late, she remembered Velma's gown. She risked a peek at Rick. He was propped on his pillow, hands behind his head, staring frankly at her.

She reached for the sheet.

"Don't." His hand snaked out and caught hers. "Let me look at you in the candlelight." He took his time, studying her as if she were a rare bird he was thinking of mounting and hanging in his trophy case. Shivers crawled over her skin.

"We forgot to blow out the candles," she said.

"I didn't forget. I thought it would be romantic to let them burn a while."

"I'm not looking for romance; I'm looking for Lucky."

"Ahhh, yes. The elusive husband." Smiling, he reached up and ran his hand lightly down her cheek. "I hope he appreciates just how lucky he is."

"Don't."

It was a token protest, and he knew it. Instead of removing his hand, he let it glide slowly down her cheek, down her throat, and across her left shoulder.

"You were made to be loved, my pet."

"Not by you." His fingertips made small circles on her skin. She felt herself go limp.

Rick exerted the lightest pressure on her shoulder, and she slid across the bed toward him. Not even a Wall of Jericho could have kept her out of his arms. It was wrong, it was not in character, and she knew she'd regret it in the morning. But only a saint or a martyr would have turned away, and she had never claimed to be either.

He ran his hands over her back, starting at the back of her neck and working all the way down to the base of her spine. There was nothing quite as erotic as the feel of a man's hands pressing through a silk garment, she thought. Her skin tingled, heated up. She was in the arms of an expert, and she knew it. She didn't even try to resist him. Besides that, the room was full of a kind of heady fragrance. It wafted from the curtains and floated around the burning candles. Martha Ann felt as if she were at the mercy of some mysterious power. And it was certainly beyond her control.

Her arms circled his shoulders and pulled him closer. His skin was warm and slightly damp with perspiration. She leaned over and nibbled his shoulder. A shudder ran through him.

He flipped her onto her back and pinned her underneath him. For a moment he remained poised above her, propped on his elbows, studying her face. Desire was there, a desire that matched his own. His mouth slammed down on hers. It was a no-holds-barred kiss, a hungry exchange by two experts who knew exactly what they wanted but didn't quite understand why.

Ahhh, he thought. She was good. More than good. She was the best. He thought her excellent rating as a lover might be due to the nightgown she was wearing. It bared enough flesh to tease and covered enough to tantalize. Wearing that gown Martha Ann Riley could have single-handedly brought the American Revolution to a standstill. Or it could be her skin. Silky, satiny, velvety. That fool poet in his soul was at it again. Or perhaps it was her lips. They were lush and inviting, and he could swear that he tasted the beauty spot.

He ran his right hand down her hips, feeling the silk gown against satin flesh. He almost lost control. His hand closed over the gown and slid it upward. She was making small murmuring sounds now. He loved a woman who voiced her pleasure.

He lifted his head just long enough for a quick breath, and then he took her lips again. He couldn't seem to get enough of her.

Martha Ann had never felt such pleasure. One of her college friends had had a rating for lovers. On a scale of one to ten, Rick was a ten plus. At first she thought his rating might be due to his chest. It was fabulous—broad and muscular with exactly the right sprinkling of crisp hair, just enough to tease a woman to distraction. Or it could be his eyes. Nothing was quite as sexy as the eyes of a man who desires a woman. His lips were top-notch, of course. She loved a man who held nothing back. He seemed to be kissing with his very soul.

She tangled her hands in his hair and pulled him closer. She couldn't seem to get enough of him.

The bedsprings started a squeaky rhythm. Ahhh, she thought. She wanted him. She had to have him. He shifted his hips and moved his hand under her gown. His touch sent shivers up her spine. She arched toward him.

He propped himself on one elbow and gazed down at her. "Martha Ann O'Grady, we're going to be good together."

Good grief, she thought. O'Grady. She was supposed to be a married woman.

"Stop right now." It was a shaky command, but a command nonetheless. If he hadn't spoken, she would have ruined her sister's reputation, right there in the Running Bear's curtained bed.

His breathing was raspy, and he was so tight with need, he thought he would explode, and she was telling him to stop? By george, that Martha Ann Riley was enough to make a man take up cussing again.

"You want me to stop? Now?"

"Yes. Just what do you think you were doing?"

"I thought *we* were doing it together."

"Not me."

"Don't tell me you were exercising your mouth again."

"No. Not exactly."

"Some other part of your anatomy, then?" His breathing was beginning to get back to normal, and his pulse was slowing down. He almost saw the funny side of the situation.

She looked up at him, then turned her head away and glanced around the room. He could tell she was trying to think up some outrageous lie. A smile tugged at the corners of his mouth.

"I couldn't help myself," she said. "I think I'm allergic to this room." She swung her gaze back to him. "Don't you think this room smells funny?"

He sniffed. "Just the candles I think." By george, he thought, Martha Ann Riley never ceased to amuse him. If any other woman had led him on like that and then left him panting at the gate, he'd probably have been mad, but it was impossible to be angry at the madcap Martha Ann.

"Would you mind moving your leg?"

"Which one? The left or the right?"

"The left, I think."

"Certainly." He lifted his left leg off her hip but kept the rest of his body pressed intimately against her. He supposed a true gentleman would have moved quickly to the other side of the bed, but he'd never pretended to be a gentleman. Anyhow, being rebuffed smarted. His small revenge would be to make her work for her freedom. "Is that better?"

"No. I think it's your other leg."

He moved it a fraction of an inch, just enough to get his weight off her but not enough to lose body contact.

"How about that?"

"Much better. Thank you." He guessed her elaborate politeness was due to guilt feelings. Or perhaps she was having as hard a time as he was coming down off the sexual high they'd been on. Smoothing her gown down over her hips, she took a deep breath. "I'm still having a hard time breathing," she said.

"Why do you think that is?"

"I believe your face is a little too close. You're taking up all my oxygen."

He put some distance between them, enough so

that four or five good-size slivered almonds could have been fitted in the space.

"Can you breathe now?"

"Yes. Thank you."

"You're welcome." He didn't try to hide his smile now. Martha Ann Riley had provided more amusement in twenty-four hours than most women would have in three months. And their trip was only beginning. He could hardly wait to see what she would do next.

Martha Ann's mind was whirling. Rick had done everything she had asked him. And he'd been polite about it all. She couldn't complain. And yet, he was still only inches from her, sending signals that made her hot all over. She had to get him on the other side of the bed—permanently.

"I do believe those candles are making me sick," she said.

"Perhaps I should blow them out."

"Would you?"

"Of course."

He sat up and stretched, deliberately, she thought, just to show his fabulous muscles. Then he pulled the curtains aside and got out of bed. She had never seen a man take so long to blow out a few candles. He lollygagged around the room, loitering over his tasks, grinning. He looked good enough to eat. She knew she could have shut her eyes, but she didn't really want to. What was the harm in looking?

He grinned at her over the last candle. "Almost done."

"Great. I feel better already."

He chuckled. "We can't have you getting sick." His bare feet padded against the floor as he made his way back to bed in the dark. The springs squeaked and the mattress sagged on his side.

Good grief, she thought. She'd gone through all that rigamarole to get him on his side of the bed, and it hadn't made a bit of difference. Distance didn't matter. Proximity did. The minute he got back into bed, she wanted to crawl over there and curl up against his chest. She had the willpower of a day-old baby bird. Shoot. What was she going to do?

"Is there anything else I can do for you, Mrs. O'Grady?"

Even his sexy voice coming out of the dark sent her blood racing. And she didn't even have her rosary to help her. She guessed she would have to rely on her brain. She lay in bed, thinking and thinking. Finally an idea dawned: Since nothing could dampen *her* ardor, she was going to cool his.

"I could use a glass of water."

"I don't think there's any left in the kitchen."

"Do you know where the pump is?"

"You want me to go out in the middle of the night and pump you a glass of water?"

"I hate to ask you, but a woman in my condition is subject to strange whims."

"And what condition is that, my pet?"

"I'm pregnant."

Six

Rick laughed all the way to the water pump. Pregnant, indeed. Her latest tale didn't deter him at all; it only made the chase more fun.

He hung the bucket on the spout and pumped some water. On his way back to the house, it splashed over the rim and onto his feet. He was careful coming back through the screen door. He didn't want to wake the entire household, and he didn't want to drip water on the floor.

The two clocks struck midnight when he walked into the kitchen, one half a second behind the other. The twenty-four beat syncopated rhythm was enough to wake his Grandma Springer, and she was so deaf she couldn't hear a one hundred-piece brass band. While he stood adjusting to the racket, an idea took hold.

His grin got bigger and bigger. He set down the bucket and walked to the refrigerator. He was sure Velma wouldn't mind if he borrowed a few things, especially since it was for such a good cause.

When he got back to the bedroom, he found Martha Ann sitting primly on her side, the sheet tucked up around her chin. That innocent pose didn't make her one bit less sexy. In fact, it only made her more appealing.

"I brought your water."

"Thank you."

"In fact, I brought a whole bucketful—in case you get thirsty in the middle of the night."

"How thoughtful."

He snapped on the light, put down his load of supplies, and poured a glass of water. She reached out her hand, but he pretended he didn't see. Instead, he came around to her side of the bed and sat down, close enough to press against her thigh.

"Here you are, my sweet." He carefully placed the glass in her right hand, then reached for her left.

"What are you doing?"

"Pampering you. My mother taught me that pregnant ladies have to be petted." He rubbed his thumb in her palm, enjoying the slight shiver that went through her. "Don't you worry, sweetheart. I intend to see that you are properly taken care of. Somebody has to do it until we find your husband."

She couldn't complain about that. There was nothing she could do except drink her water and endure his petting. After she had finished drinking, he took the glass and put it carefully on the bedside table beside six brass candlesticks.

"Thanks. That was very refreshing." He was still sitting on her side of the bed. Close. "You can go to sleep now."

"Not yet. I have something for you."

"I don't need anything else, thank you."

"You don't have to pretend with me. I know all about pregnant women." He reached over to the bedside table and picked up a plate. "It's bad for the baby to let these cravings go unattended." He held the plate under her nose.

"What is that?"

"A pickle and ice-cream sandwich."

"A pickle and ice-cream sandwich?" The smell alone turned her stomach upside down. "How in the world did you do that?"

"It was simple. I sliced two big kosher dills and spread the chocolate ice cream between them. I was certain Velma wouldn't mind." He picked up the awful concoction and held it to her lips. "Here, sweetheart, let me help you."

"I'm really not craving that yet. It's too early in my pregnancy."

"Great. We'll nip it in the bud before it ever gets started. Here, my sweet. Take a bite."

She nibbled the edge of the pickle, trying not to get any of the chocolate ice cream at the same time.

"There," he said. "Is that better?"

"Umhph." The pickle sandwich was worse than she had imagined. She wondered if she could plead a call of nature and spit the stuff out. But knowing Rick, he'd insist on accompanying her, especially since the bathroom was an outdoor facility halfway between the house and the barn.

She decided the lesser of two evils was staying in the bed. She took another bite of his odious offering, just to back up her story, and then she pushed it aside.

"I couldn't eat another bite."

He held it back under her nose. "I insist. You have to keep up your strength."

"I'm . . . watching my weight." She pushed the pickle and ice-cream sandwich away with one hand. "It's bad to gain too much weight during a pregnancy."

"In that case, I might as well throw this away and come back to bed."

Her false pregnancy didn't make things one bit better. The minute he was back in bed, every nerve in her body was tingling. She thought she would never go to sleep.

It was the smell that woke Martha Ann up early the next morning. She sat up in bed and took a deep breath. The scent made her nostrils burn.

"Good grief. What is that?"

Rick had his face buried in the pillow. "Did you say something?" he mumbled.

"There's a strange smell in this room. It smells like sour food."

He lifted his head off the pillow and sniffed. "By george, I think you're right. I wonder if I dropped any pickle juice on the floor."

Martha Ann threw back the covers and swung her feet to the floor, and then she remembered her nightgown. She jerked the sheet around herself, uncovering Rick. Dressed in his shorts, with the early morning sunlight gilding his skin, he was a sight to see. She had a hard time not looking. And he noticed.

He chuckled. "Let's work out a method for this."

"What do you suggest?"

"You get out on that side of the bed, and I'll get out on this side. We'll keep our backs to each other. That way we can save time dressing and preserve your modesty."

"What about your modesty?"

"I have none."

The bed squeaked as they both got up and reached for their clothes. Martha Ann silently thanked Velma for having folded her clothes and left them in the room. They kept their bargain, turning their backs and dressing quickly. But it wasn't quick enough for Martha Ann. Her awareness of Rick McGill took precedence over everything else. She had to button her blouse twice before she got it right. He couldn't seem to do anything quietly. He was over there whistling and humming and chuckling to himself as if he were watching old Laurel and Hardy movies instead of putting on his pants and shirt. She just knew he was up to something.

She was tucking her blouse into her jeans when she heard his roar.

"What in the devil is this?"

She whirled around and saw him emerging from underneath the bed, holding his nose with one hand and a mesh bag with the other.

"Good grief. What is that stuff?"

"It smells like a malodorous cow. Stand away from the window, Martha Ann." He started around the bed, holding the bag well out in front of him.

"What are you going to do?"

"First I'm going to get this stinking concoction out of here, then I'm going outside and give it a decent burial."

He opened the window and tossed out the bag.

It landed at Clyde's feet. He'd gone out to feed the chickens, and at first he thought one of his hens had finally decided to lay an egg.

"Good girl, Belinda."

Belinda ruffled her feathers and pecked his shin. Clyde bent over to rub his leg and saw the mesh bag.

"My gosh, it's my love potion."

He picked the bag up and hurried into the house. Velma was standing at the stove breaking eggs into a skillet.

"Look what I found, Velma, Right out there in the dirt." Clyde held the bag aloft.

"Shoot, Clyde. How did it get out there?"

"I guess one of them found it under the bed and tossed it out without knowing what it was."

"Reckon it was there long enough to do the trick?"

"I don't know. This love potion is supposed to be quick acting. Of course, I had to change the formula some. It could be that it will take a little longer."

"Well, put it back, Clyde."

"How can I do that? They're still in the bedroom."

"When they come out, you sneak back in there and put that love potion right back under the bed."

"Good morning." Velma and Clyde jumped at the sound of Rick's voice. Clyde hid the love potion behind his back as Rick and Martha Ann walked into the kitchen.

"Did you sleep well?" Velma asked.

"Great." Rick and Martha Ann lied at the same time, then looked sheepishly at each other.

"Breakfast will be ready in a minute." Velma turned to her eggs which had gone beyond golden and were turning a rusty brown.

"I'm not very hungry this morning," Martha Ann said. "Do you mind if I pass?"

"A good spot of fresh air might do you good." Rick took her elbow. "If you don't mind, Velma, we'll take a short walk. If you have any eggs left, we'll eat them, and then we'll clean up the kitchen for you."

Velma winked at Clyde. "That sounds like a wonderful idea."

Rick and Martha Ann hurried out the door. When the screen had closed behind them, Velma turned to Clyde.

"Quick, Clyde. Put the potion back under the bed. I think it's working."

. . .

Rick and Martha Ann didn't stop walking until they had reached the cottonwood tree beside the barn.

"Good grief. The whole house smells like that." She fanned her face with her hand.

"Do you suppose it's Velma's cooking?"

"Why would her food be in a bag under the bed?"

"Beats me. Maybe Clyde was saving some for a midnight snack and forgot about it." He walked to the barn and picked up the shovel that was leaning beside the door. "Do you want to watch me bury the stuff?"

"Yes. I won't breathe easy until I know it's six feet under the ground."

Rick laughed and flexed his muscles. "Granted, I do have muscles, my dear. But I wasn't planning to bury it quite that deep."

Laughing, they walked across the yard until they came to a spot a few feet from their bedroom window.

"The bag should be here somewhere." Rick kicked a few corncobs out of the way. Belinda and the rest of the chickens clucked angrily at him.

"How far did you toss it?"

"Not far."

They spent ten minutes searching for the lost bag. Finally they gave up and carried the shovel back to the barn.

"Where do you suppose the bag is?" Martha Ann asked.

"It doesn't matter. At least it's not in our bedroom."

They went back inside to do the breakfast dishes. Clyde and Velma showed them the leftover eggs, and then excused themselves to work in the vegetable garden.

As soon as the Running Bears were out of ear-shot, Rick turned to Martha Ann.

"Are you feeling all right?"

"Certainly. I'm going to find Velma's dish washing liquid." She bent over and began to search the lower cabinets. "I'm sure she keeps it here somewhere."

She felt two large hands circle her waist. "What in the world are you doing? A woman in your condition should not be doing dishes."

"Good grief. I'm perfectly fine. Just a little pregnant."

He laughed. "How does one become a little pregnant, Martha Ann?"

With a little lie, she thought. But she certainly didn't say that. She stayed bent over, searching for the dish washing liquid. His hands were still around her waist, in fact, they were massaging her torso in a wonderfully exciting way. She thanked her favorite saint that she was wearing her own clothes today instead of Velma's exotic harem outfit that bared about four square feet of skin. Gracious, if Rick McGill only knew what he did to her! She stuck her head further under the sink and took a long, steadying breath.

"My husband did it."

"What did you say?" Rick moved closer. The back of her legs were now pressed intimately against the front of his. "I can't hear you with your head under the sink."

"Never mind." She couldn't stay under the sink forever. Sooner or later she'd have to come out and face Rick. She began to back out, bottle in hand. He still had his hands around her waist.

When she started to straighten up, Rick turned her expertly so that she was in his arms, face-to-face with him. Pamper, indeed, she thought. That was just another word for seduce. As incredible as it seemed, he was not above trying to seduce a pregnant woman. He was a scoundrel through and through. But, oh my. Standing in his arms she almost sighed. Why did he have to be such a lovable scoundrel?

"Here, let me take that." His voice was soft as he plucked the dish washing liquid out of her hands and set it on the kitchen counter. "We can't have you exerting yourself."

"There's really no need for all this. I'm perfectly fine." Her protest was weak, and she knew it. Being in Rick's arms did that to her. She lost most of her sense and all of her willpower.

"I'll have to find out for myself." He gently caressed the side of her throat. "Checking your pulse." His dark eyes twinkled with devilment. "It's a little fast. I do believe I'm going to have to take you to bed."

"Take me to bed?"

"To rest. What did you think I meant?"

"Naturally that's what I thought you meant."

His hand was still on her throat. Now he moved it up to cup her cheek. "Your face is flushed. Do you think that's significant?"

"It just means I'm a little hot." She was hot all right, but not from any physical condition, unless you could count terminal bad judgment of men.

"You are?" He smiled his devilish smile again.

"Perhaps I should sit down." She would use any excuse to get out of her present predicament.

"An excellent idea." Befofe she knew what was happening, Rick had scooped her up in his arms and was carrying her toward a rocking chair. "We can't have you on your feet too much."

"This is perfectly ridiculous. Put me down."

"I'd ruin my reputation if I did."

"And what reputation is that? Chasing married women?"

"How you wound me, my pet." He chuckled. "Actually, it's the reputation of the entire McGill clan. We're known far and wide for the exquisite care we take of pregnant women." He kissed her cheek. "Don't worry, sweetheart. I'm going to take good care of you until we find your lost husband."

She had created a monster. Why couldn't he be the type of man who was scared to death of pregnant women?

"That's what I'm afraid of," she muttered.

"Did you say something, my sweet?"

"I said, 'The chair is right there.' You can put me down."

"Do you think I'd put you in a chair without checking it out first? And you in your condition?" He sat down in the rocking chair, arranged her in his lap, and began to rock. "Hmmm . . . ahhh, yes." He pulled her a little closer. "This does quite nicely. . . . Yes, indeed."

She had never before had the urge to make love in a rocking chair. But she did now. The rocking motion of the chair and the intimacy of sitting on his lap gave her notions she didn't want to be having.

"Hmmmm." She leaned her head against his shoulder.

"You like that, do you?"

"Ahhh, yes. . . ." She closed her eyes, inhaling the clean masculine scent of him.

He tipped her chin up with one finger. She opened her eyes in time to see him lowering his mouth toward hers.

"No." Her protest was weak and then louder. "NO!"

With his mouth only a fraction of an inch from hers, he asked, "What's the matter? Did you think I

was going to kiss you?" His warm breath stirred
against her cheek.

"Weren't you?"

"No. I was checking your face for signs of fatigue.
Pregnant women tire easily."

"How could I possibly be tired? You won't even let
me walk across the floor by myself."

"You have to save your strength."

"For what?"

"For the baby." He stood up and deposited her
carefully in the chair. "Wait right there, my pet."

She thought of leaving but there was nowhere to
go except to the bedroom or outside. She certainly
didn't want to be cornered in the bedroom with
Rick. The night to come was soon enough for another trial by fire in that chamber of love. And if she
went outside, she was sure to get caught up in
another of Clyde's and Velma's matchmaking schemes.
She decided to wait in the chair to see what Rick
would come up with next.

"Here, my pet. Drink your milk."

She'd been so busy thinking, she hadn't noticed
what he was doing. Now he stood in front of her
holding a very tall, very full glass of milk. She hated
milk.

"I don't want it."

"Don't you want your baby to have healthy bones
and teeth? I insist." He held the glass to her lips.

She took a small sip and made a face. It was worse
than she had expected.

Rick pretended not to notice. He put the glass in
her hand and dragged up a stool for her feet.

"Comfortable, my sweet?" He didn't wait for a reply. "I'll do the dishes while you drink your milk."

He went to the kitchen counter whistling. He was
thoroughly enjoying this latest episode with the men-

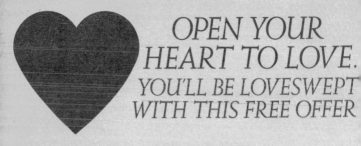

OPEN YOUR HEART TO LOVE.
YOU'LL BE LOVESWEPT WITH THIS FREE OFFER

HERE'S WHAT YOU GET:

1. FREE! SIX NEW LOVESWEPT NOVELS! You get 6 beautiful stories filled with passion, romance, laughter, and tears... exciting romances to stir the excitement of falling in love... again and again.

2. FREE! A BEAUTIFUL MAKEUP CASE WITH A MIRROR THAT LIGHTS UP! What could be more useful than a makeup case with a mirror that lights up*? Once you open the tortoise-shell finish case, you have a choice of brushes... for your lips, your eyes, and your blushing cheeks.

*(batteries not included)

3. SAVE! MONEY-SAVING HOME DELIVERY! Join the Loveswept at-home reader service and we'll send you 6 new novels each month. You always get 15 days to preview them before you decide. Each book is yours for only $2.09 — a savings of 41¢ per book.

4. BEAT THE CROWDS! You'll always receive your Loveswept books before they are available in bookstores. You'll be the first to thrill to these exciting new stories.

BE LOVESWEPT TODAY — JUST COMPLETE, DETACH AND MAIL YOUR FREE-OFFER CARD.

FREE–LIGHTED MAKEUP CASE!
FREE–6 LOVESWEPT NOVELS!

- NO OBLIGATION
- NO PURCHASE NECESSARY

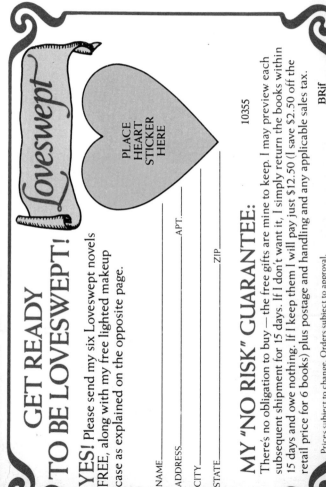

GET READY TO BE LOVESWEPT!

YES! Please send my six Loveswept novels FREE, along with my free lighted makeup case as explained on the opposite page.

NAME_____

ADDRESS_____APT.____

CITY_____

STATE_____ZIP_____

PLACE HEART STICKER HERE

10355

MY "NO RISK" GUARANTEE:

There's no obligation to buy — the free gifts are mine to keep. I may preview each subsequent shipment for 15 days. If I don't want it, I simply return the books within 15 days and owe nothing. If I keep them I will pay just $12.50 (I save $2.50 off the retail price for 6 books) plus postage and handling and any applicable sales tax.

BRjf

Prices subject to change. Orders subject to approval.

REMEMBER!

- The free books and gift are mine to keep!
- There is no obligation!
- I may preview each shipment for 15 days!
- I can cancel anytime!

dacious Mrs. Lucky O'Grady. He put a pan of water on to heat and glanced over his shoulder at Martha Ann. She was sipping and frowning as if she had a glass of motor oil in her hand. He had an attack of conscience, but it was only a small one. He supposed he'd exacted enough revenge for her latest lie. It had all been in fun anyway. Except the kisses. They had started out as fun, but somewhere between the Valley of Fire and the curtain-draped bedroom they had turned into something else. He poured the hot water into the dishpan as he tried to analyze exactly what Martha Ann Riley's kisses had become. Sweet. Delicious. Hot. Steamy. The few words were apt but entirely inadequate. How could a man describe something that seemed to touch his soul? he wondered.

He glanced at her again. She looked serene sitting in the rocking chair with her feet propped up. She was no longer making any pretense of sipping the milk; she was merely staring into space, a half-smile on her lips. He almost believed in the myth of her pregnancy. She glowed, she had the look. What would it be like to have a pregnant wife? To know that a woman was carrying his child? It was something he'd never thought of before. He'd only thought in terms of his fun and his freedom. Even when he'd considered that he would someday settle down, he hadn't thought of having children.

As he turned his attention back to the dishes, his best friend came into mind. If ever there was a man who adored his wife and family, it was Jacob Donovan. He was the same old devil-may-care, quick-to-laugh Jacob, but these days he was settling for supervising his oil field fire fighters instead of being in the thick of the blaze himself. That and full-time doting. If ever a man doted, it was Jacob. To hear him tell it, his two boys, Benjamin and Joseph, were the smartest, brightest children in Greenville. His wife Rachel, in the eighth month of her pregnancy with twins, had confided that Jacob was spoiling all of them.

She adored it, of course. That Rachel Donovan was some woman.

Martha Ann was like her in some ways—full of fun and spirit, given to quick laughter and quick passions. Jacob Donovan had fallen under Rachel's spell not once, but twice. Rick decided that it might behoove him to exercise a little caution around Martha Ann. He had no intention of falling under anybody's spell, and he certainly had no intention of settling into domestic bliss this early in his life.

"The dishes are all done, my sweet. I think I'll take another look at that tractor. Maybe I can get it running."

Rick left the kitchen with unusual haste. Martha Ann told herself she should be relieved. No more pampering and no more steamy caresses. She left the rocking chair and put the unfinished glass of milk in the refrigerator. It would be there in case Rick wanted to force more calcium on her.

Together the two clocks on the wall struck twenty. Only ten o'clock. Twelve more hours until she had to climb into that bed again with Rick McGill. She figured she would use the time wisely by shoring up her weakened defenses. And the only way she knew how to do that was to avoid seeing him.

She went outside, found Velma, and lined up enough chores to last her until nighttime.

That evening she was in bed long before Rick. Pleading tiredness, she'd gone to bed early, leaving him watching a sitcom and a detective show with the Running Bears.

The first thing she noticed when she went into the bedroom was the smell. Good grief, she thought. Not again. She turned on the light and searched the room. Sure enough, the little mesh bag was right back under the bed. She picked it up gingerly and tossed it back out the window. The only way she knew to get rid of the smell was to light the scented candles. So she did. All of them.

When he came into the room, she was lying flat on her back, staring at the ceiling, surrounded by gossamer curtains and blazing candles.

"I see you've prepared for me."

"Oh, hush up and come to bed." During the day she'd washed Velma's clothes at the creek, helped her can six quarts of tomatoes, and learned to needlepoint. But it hadn't helped one bit in getting Rick McGill out of her mind. She was tired, and she was testy.

"Eager, are you, my pet?" His clothes hit the floor with a plop, and he climbed in beside her.

"If you so much as put one foot on my side of the bed, I'll scream."

"You shouldn't scare a fellow like that."

"Humph." She flopped over and turned her back to him.

"Good night, my pet." He reached over and patted her bottom.

She jumped at his touch. He chuckled.

"Muscle spasms," she said. "You had nothing to do with it."

"I'll have to try harder next time."

"I keep hoping there won't be a next time."

"Haven't you noticed. There always is with us."

He turned on his side, facing her, and his hand

flopped casually onto her shoulder. She pretended not to notice.

So did he. She was just an ordinary woman, he told himself. Extraordinarily good-looking, to be sure. And warm and spirited and funny. But still, she was only a passing amusement. So why did he feel as if electric currents were running from her skin through his hand? He wasn't going to move it though. He didn't want her to think that *he* thought of her as anything except a quarry.

He shut his eyes and tried to sleep.

So did she. He was just another man of the wrong kind, she told herself. Extremely good-looking, of course. And warm and bright and funny. But still, he was only a temporary amusement, a little added spice in her life while she was finding Lucky. Then why did the merest touch of his hand make her feel as if she were melting? She wasn't going to move though. She didn't want him to think that *she* thought of him as anything except a means of finding her make-believe husband.

The minutes ticked by. They lay stiffly side by side, barely touching but feeling as if they were locked in a full body press with each other. It was exquisite torture. She was torn between hoping he would pull her into his arms and wanting to roll out of his reach. He was torn between turning his back to her and pinning her beneath him on the sagging mattress and giving vent to his passion.

She shut her eyes and counted the number of times he had kissed her. He stared at the ceiling and counted the number of times he could have had her and didn't.

She decided that she was hopelessly addicted to scoundrels.

He decided that he was in grave danger of losing his freedom.

Finally she spoke. "You forgot to blow out the candles."

It was the excuse he needed to move his hand off her shoulder without seeming too obvious about it. He jumped out of bed with such alacrity, the bedsprings vibrated.

That's all she needed, Martha Ann thought. A vibrating bed. In her state of mind, though, any relief was welcome. She tried not to notice Rick as he marched around the room in his shorts blowing out candles. But how could she help herself? He was so good-looking.

At last the room was dark, and he came back to bed. This time he was excruciatingly careful not to touch her. And finally they both slept.

The next morning Martha Ann got out of bed and dressed before Rick was even awake. Holding her shoes in her hand, she tiptoed out the door. Once she'd closed the door, she leaned against it and took a deep breath. She'd gotten through the night without a close encounter. She didn't think she could get through one more night in that bed without some help. She had to figure out a plan.

When the clocks struck twenty that night, Martha Ann excused herself and went to bed. But she wasn't going there to sleep. On the contrary, she thought. She was going to prepare for one more trial by fire with Rick McGill.

When he came through the door thirty minutes

later, he was grinning. His grin broadened when he saw Martha Ann.

She was sitting on her side of the bed wearing a voluminous pink flowered bedsheet and half a pound of cold cream. Skeins of thread were piled in the middle of the bed making a brightly colored Wall of Jericho. She was working away on a piece of needlepoint, and he thought she was smiling. Under all that cold cream it was hard to tell.

He leaned against the door frame and prepared to enjoy the show.

"What are you doing, my pet?"

"Knitting."

She caught her tongue between her teeth as she concentrated on pulling a needle and thread through the needlepoint canvas.

"Where are your knitting needles?"

Oh, heck, she thought. He knew the difference between knitting and needlepoint. Never mind. She'd wing it.

"Did I say 'knitting'? I meant needlepoint."

He moved around to her side of the bed and sat down, taking great care to sit on her flowered bedsheet. He noted with satisfaction that his weight strained the knot she'd tied over her shoulder and flattened the sheet against her breasts. There was nothing Martha Ann Riley could do to make herself unattractive. Still, he was flattered that she'd bothered to try. It meant she was having a hard time resisting him. And that's just the way he liked it.

"Do you mind if I watch? This kind of work fascinates me."

"Of course not." Was there nothing that would discourage this man she wondered. She pushed the wretched needle through the stubborn canvas and tangled a knot as big as Texas. When she tried to untangle it, it got even bigger. She wished Rick wouldn't sit so close. She wished he wasn't so attractive. She wished she didn't like wicked men.

"Here. Let me." He took the canvas from her and deftly untangled the knot. Then he stuck the needle neatly into the cloth and handed it to her. "That's an intriguing pattern, butterflies and daisies. What are you making?"

"Booties."

"Booties?" He didn't bother to hide his laughter.

"Yes. For Michael."

"Who's Michael?"

"The baby."

"Of course." He patted her flat stomach and then didn't bother to move his hand. "How could I forget the baby?"

That big suntanned hand on the flowered sheet sent heat waves through her body. She tried to concentrate on the needlepoint but only succeeded in tangling another knot.

Without a word he took the canvas and began to straighten it out again. "Needlepointed booties. With daisies and butterflies. Don't you think Michael might be embarrassed to wear them to the nursery?"

"He's going to be an unusual baby."

Rick patted her stomach and grinned. "He's definitely an unusual baby."

"He's going to take after his father Lucky the Gambler."

"I think he's more likely to take after his mother Martha Ann the actress."

"Actress?"

"Yes. You're the mistress of pretense, and I love every minute of it." He reached across her, scooped up the thread, and dumped it on the bedside table.

Then he lifted the needlepoint canvas out of her hands and dropped it on top of the thread.

"What are you doing?"

"I felt a sudden desire for a facial." With one swift move he lay down beside her and pulled her on top of him. His hands cupped her face and brought it down to his. The cold cream made their lips slick. It only enhanced their passion.

"Hmmmm, delicious," he said. He rubbed his cheek against hers, slicking his face and nose with cream. Holding her face between his hands, he nibbled her earlobe and planted hot kisses down the side of her throat.

The knot loosened, and her sheet slipped down, baring her chest. His tongue traced the tops of her breasts.

"Please," she whispered.

"Happy to oblige." He rolled over, taking her with him. Her hair was tousled, and her blue eyes were enormous. The cold cream was now divided equally between them, leaving her with only a slight sheen on her face. Sexy, he thought. There was nothing sexier than a naked, fresh-faced woman in a sheet.

He took her mouth again. She wrapped her arms around him and began to rock. Their passion spiraled. Both fought to control it.

"Just to . . . show you . . . that . . . nothing . . . can . . . discourage me." He spoke between kisses. His breathing was harsh and uneven.

"Just so . . . you . . . know . . . that . . . I'm merely . . . obliging . . . because I'm . . . too much . . . of a lady . . . to fight." Her fingernails dug into his back. The rhythm of her hips teased him.

"In that case . . ." He lifted his head and gazed down at her. That black hair spread across the pillow, and those enormous blue eyes were almost his undoing. ". . . we might as well make this good."

They kissed until their lips felt bruised and puffy. Finally Rick lifted his head and smiled down at her.

"You do your best acting in bed, my pet."

"But I don't do curtain calls." She smoothed her hair and pulled at her sheet. She was lying, of course. She'd do curtain calls all night with Rick McGill. He was that kind of man, and she was that kind of woman.

"I could easily check that out."

She hoped he wouldn't. Her sister's reputation was already in tatters, and her own was not much better. Good grief. Just to think that she had believed a little needlepoint would stop Rick McGill.

"If you want to have Michael's booties on your conscience, go ahead."

"Far be it from me to deprive that little guy of his booties." Laughing, he got off the bed and handed her the needlepoint hoop. "By all means, finish your work." He leaned down and nuzzled her ear. "But don't overdo it, my pet. You need to save your strength."

"For what?"

"Las Vegas."

He started undressing, grinning and whistling and carrying on in his usual flamboyant manner. Rick McGill never did anything without fanfare. She didn't even bother to shut her eyes. What was the use? Closing her eyes so she wouldn't see the body she'd practically been mauling seemed the height of hypocrisy.

He finished undressing and climbed into bed. She took up her needle and punched the canvas. She was determined to work until he fell asleep. That way she might avoid another close encounter with temptation.

Goodness gracious, she thought. He felt just right over there on that side of the bed—a good solid bulk making the mattress sag in all the right places, a warm comforting presence as inviting as a woolen blanket on a thirty-degree night.

She tangled another knot in her thread and had to cut it out with the scissors. Turning her head, she sneaked a peek at Rick. He had his eyes closed, but he was grinning. She wondered what he had meant by saving her strength for Las Vegas.

Seven

The next morning Clyde Running Bear's pickup truck was delivered.

With the two clocks chiming and the two televisions going and Velma practicing her dance steps and packing a picnic basket and Clyde running in and out banging the screen door behind him, preparations were made for the journey to Las Vegas.

The four of them set out for the wicked city at ten o'clock that morning. Velma and Clyde rode up front in royal splendor. He had donned an elaborately beaded headband for the occasion, and she was dressed in her blondest wig, her longest false eyelashes, and her flashiest blouse.

Rick and Martha Ann sat in the pickup bed on two straight chairs. They rode backward, the backs of their chairs braced against the cab. The chairs had been Clyde's idea.

The old pickup roared and rattled as Clyde nursed it down the road at a breakneck speed of forty miles an hour. Conversation was difficult in the back of the truck but not impossible.

"Are you comfortable?" Rick shouted.

"Yes." The wind whipped Martha Ann's hair around her face as she turned to him. "I haven't ridden in the back of a pickup truck since I was fifteen. I'd forgotten what fun it is."

A late model Chevy with Florida license plates passed them. Three children in the backseat pointed their fingers and grinned.

Rick and Martha Ann waved at them.

"You don't mind being a tourist attraction?" Rick asked.

"It's easier than being pregnant."

Rick roared with laughter. "It certainly is. Especially in your situation."

"I've been in so many situations lately, I'm hard-pressed to know which one you're talking about."

"No husband."

"Ah, yes. My lost husband." She held her hair back from her face with one hand. "Everything will be better when we find him."

"Sweetheart, if things get any better, I won't be responsible for what I do."

"If you're referring to that bed in *The Arabian Nights,* let me remind you that we'll have separate beds from now on."

"Separate beds have never been a hindrance to me." He winked at her. "As a matter of fact, neither have separate chairs." He scooted his chair close and plucked her off her chair like a vine-ripe tomato. Then he arranged her on his lap with the finesse of a man who knew how to cuddle.

"You put me down."

"I can't have you bouncing around over there on that hard-bottomed chair, little Mama." He patted her stomach. "It's not good for Michael." He wasn't behaving at all, and neither was his hand. It was roaming over her torso, poking and probing at her blouse. His index finger slipped into the space between the buttonholes and found her warm flesh.

"If I weren't afraid of falling out of the truck, I'd get up and whack you in the nose."

"I'm terrified." He laughed.

"You're a blade."

"That too."

"Just wait till I get you to Las Vegas."

"Promises, promises."

Inside the cab, Velma pressed her nose against the window and looked back.

"She's sitting on his lap, Clyde."

"I knew those chairs were just the thing. I'm glad I thought of them."

"The chairs were my idea."

"It's the love potion working."

"Where is it?"

"I found it out in the yard again."

"Oh, no."

"Don't worry, honey. I dusted it off and tucked it into that sack full of stuff you gave Martha Ann. I put it right in there between the deodorant and the shampoo."

Still looking back, Velma reached over and clutched Clyde's arm. "I believe he's going to kiss her . . . yes, he's got his hand on her face . . . he's leaning closer . . . closer. Oh, my. Oh, NO!"

"What is it, Velma? What happened?"

"I do believe Martha Ann pinched his ear. Just like a schoolmarm."

"Don't worry about it, honey. The more they want it, the harder to get they play."

She pressed her face so close to the glass, her nose squashed in. She stayed that way a few minutes without speaking, then she turned back around, smiling.

"Well?" The truck swerved as Clyde swiveled his head to look at Velma.

"She might have pinched his ear with one hand, but she's rubbing the back of his neck with the other."

"Maybe they'll name the first baby after me."

It took two hours to get to Las Vegas. Clyde delivered them to one of the smaller hotels on the Strip, The Orchid, and they said their good-byes. Martha Ann hugged them and promised to write, and Rick shook their hands and privately decided that as soon as he got home he would arrange a little surprise for the Running Bears—indoor plumbing.

Clyde and Velma climbed back into their pickup truck and pulled onto the Strip. Velma leaned out the window and waved until they were out of sight.

Rick turned to Martha Ann. "This is it, kiddo."

"Just look at us." She spread her arms wide. "We're both covered with forty miles of desert dust. And we have nothing except the clothes on our backs."

"We have the modern miracle of plastic." He grinned. "You're forgetting my credit card." He took her hand. "Come on. Let's go check in."

"Separate rooms."

"Would I do anything else?"

"You would do whatever you thought you could get by with."

"Mrs. O'Grady, I can promise that you will have a palatial suite all your own, complete with telephone and running water."

"I can hardly wait."

Fifteen minutes later Rick and Martha Ann were moving into their rooms—adjoining rooms.

"Did you have to do that?"

"Lucky would never forgive me if I didn't keep close watch on you."

"Just thank your fairy godmother I'm not planning to tell him how close."

Rick stuck the key into his lock. "I'll see you after a while, Martha Ann. I have things to do."

"So do I. I may never get out of the tub." She pushed open her door and entered the blessed coolness of a room with a telephone, running water, and a bed she could call her own.

First she stripped off all her clothes. She'd have to wash them again. They were the only clothes she had. If she put the blouse over the air-conditioning vent it would be dry in a few hours. She'd have to wear the jeans damp—that was, if she could get back into them.

Small matter, she thought. She was in Las Vegas, and she'd soon find Lucky and head back home. Damp clothes would be only a minor inconvenience compared to the trials of the last few days.

She worked up a lather on the blouse and smiled. Adventure was a better word than trials. Trials were endured and adventure was enjoyed. And she'd enjoyed every minute of being with that rapscallion Rick McGill.

She draped her clothes over a chair in front of the air-conditioning vent and ran herself a tubful of hot water. Reaching into the sack of toiletries Velma had given her, she pulled out some bubble bath, a bottle of shampoo, and a small mesh bag.

"Good grief. Not again." The little bag was the worst for wear. It had a few tears where the chickens had pecked it, and it was covered with dirt from its many journeys to the backyard. And it smelled worse than ever.

"Whatever you are, good-bye forever." Martha Ann threw it into the garbage can and set the can out in the hall for the maid. Then she climbed into the tub for a long leisurely soak.

She lathered herself from head to toe, humming and singing and generally having fun. A long while later she emerged from the tub and draped herself in a towel.

She leaned over, shook her wet hair out, fluffed it up with her fingers, and stepped into her bedroom. Rick McGill was in one of her wing chairs, bold as you please, his feet propped on the bedside table. He was grinning.

She didn't even attempt to feign surprise. Nothing he did surprised her anymore.

"You're too late," she said. "I've already had my bath."

"So I see." He took time to give her a thorough perusal. "Might I add that you look good enough to eat."

"By all means. You're welcome to say anything you like as long as you stay on that side of the room."

"What's the matter? Afraid of a few sparks?"

"No. I'm afraid of getting dirty again. I'm clean, and you're still dusty from the journey." She inched toward the bed, being careful to keep the bottom of her towel together. If she could get the bedspread off, she could cover herself. "By the way, how did you get in?"

"With this." He held up an extra key to her room. "I like to cover all the bases."

"That's not all you like to cover."

He laughed. "That's true. I've spent the last hour thinking about covering that delectable body of yours." He lowered his feet and reached for a box. "Here, sweetheart, this is for you." He held the box toward her.

"What is it?"

"I've been shopping. I took the trusty plastic and bought us a couple of clean outfits."

"You bought clothes for me?"

"Nothing personal. I'll add them to your tab."

"Naturally."

He'd made it sound like a business deal, but she couldn't help being pleased. As she took the box from him, she decided that Rick could really be a nice guy when he tried. Buying her clothes. Now that was thoughtful.

"Thank you, Rick."

She looked so pleased standing there, he thought. All scrubbed and shiny in that towel, like a girl of sweet sixteen who's thinking of hugging her favorite uncle. A man could grow accustomed to having a woman like Martha Ann around the house. It wouldn't do to get too sentimental. Sentimentality was a dangerous state for a man who was already on the verge of losing his head.

He leaned back in his chair and propped his feet on the table in a deliberate gesture of nonchalance. He'd have to remedy the situation.

"I always expect payment, Martha Ann. Starting now."

She held the box in front of her chest. "I suppose I could call my bank at home to wire me some money."

"I'm not talking about money."

Her face grew wary. "What are you talking about then?"

"A performance. You're good at that."

"So are you. For a moment there, you had me thinking you were a nice guy."

"Nice guys don't have fun. And I intend to have fun." He folded his hands behind his head and leaned further back in his chair. "I want a fashion show, Mrs. O'Grady."

"A fashion show?"

"I paid for the goods; I want to see you model them."

She thought about banging the box over his head and telling him exactly what he could do with the goods. Then she changed her mind. Why not? She might just give the arrogant skunk more than he bargained for.

She carried her box into the bathroom and opened the lid. Inside was a red miniskirt with a long zipper up the front from hem to waist and a red halter top that was barely big enough to cover the principal parts, let alone the subject. A tall pair of spiky red high heels and black mesh stockings completed the outfit. He'd even thought to buy lingerie—G-string panties and a bra with holes over the nipples.

"That devil." She held the skimpy costume in front of herself and looked in the mirror. She looked like a hooker. Wasn't that just like Rick McGill to select clothes appropriate for one of the girls in his houses of ill repute? Good grief. She lowered the toilet seat cover and sat down, trying to think what to do. Obviously he expected her to be appalled by the clothes. It was his way of letting her know what he really thought of her. Well, if he thought she was 'that kind of girl,' why disappoint him? Why not give him his money's worth and then some?

She put on the stockings and lingerie then squeezed into the tight skirt and skimpy halter. Next she dug into Velma's bag of goodies and painted a slash of red across her lips. Using the same red lipstick, she made her cheeks look like two stop signs. There was nothing she could do with her hair. It was as thick and shiny as a Kentucky Derby winner's tail, and it absolutely defied taming. She shook her head and fluffed her hair out in wild disarray. The love-for-hire look. That's what she was after.

She started toward the door, then took one last look at herself. She'd forgotten about the naughty zipper on her skirt. Taking hold, she jerked it upward until it had bared her thigh almost all the way to indecency.

There, she thought. She was ready. Grinning, she pushed open the door and walked into the bedroom.

Rick McGill almost fell off his chair.

By getting that sleazy outfit he had hoped to put Martha Ann Riley back in her proper place—current playgirl. But she wouldn't stay. Even in those hooker clothes she looked like somebody's kid sister playing dress up. What was even worse, with that chin lifted high and those blue eyes blazing, she elicited an admiration that bordered on adoration. By george, he'd better be careful or he was going to get caught in his own trap.

He tried to look cool and Humphrey Bogartish and totally unaffected. "Well, sweetheart. How do you like the outfit?"

"I love it!" She twirled around, making sure she showed him everything she had. She noted with satisfaction that his breathing got heavy. "It's just what I would have chosen for myself." She stopped in front of him, close enough so that her legs were brushing against his. Then, bending at the waist and leaning over in the manner of a practiced hooker, she pressed her red lips against his. "Thank you," she murmured. She even toyed around in his mouth with her tongue.

By george, he thought, if it was an act, it was her best yet. Those hot red lips moved over his until he thought nothing could keep him from throwing her across the bed and hiking up that sleazy skirt. He already knew what was under there—that fool G-string he'd bought. Whatever had possessed him? When

her tongue slid into his mouth, he had to grip
and chair arms to keep from making a fool o
himself.

It wouldn't do to make love to her in his condi
tion. He might lose his head—and his heart.

Fortunately for his sanity, she ended the kiss and
walked back across the room. She had A-number
one, first-class hips. When she spun back around
he noticed her lips were pouty from the kiss.

Smiling, she put her hand on her skirt zipper
"What do you think? Is the zipper high enough?
She inched it up a fraction.

"I believe so." Was that his voice, he wondered. He
sounded like a bullfrog in heat.

"Of course, I don't want to be too bold. My condi
tion, you know."

"Yes." In his condition, speaking was a mino
miracle.

"But I do think this zipper could come up som
more." She gave it another tug. Rick caught a glimpse
of the black lace G-string. "I believe if you've got it
you might as well flaunt it. Right?" She spun around
and flaunted it.

"I believe the zipper's a little too high."

"What did you say?" She posed, hands on hips
legs spread apart, showing just a glimpse of black
lace.

"I said I think . . ." He got out of his chair so
quickly, it scooted backward. "Have you seen the
view from the window?" He turned around and stud
ied the horizon as if his life depended on it. "You
can see the Mountain of the Rising Sun over there
in the east."

"Where?" She came across the room, gloating a
the success of her plan. Rick McGill had gotten more
than he had bargained for all right. He was so up

tight, he looked as if he would twang if anybody touched him. She edged around the table and inched around in front of Rick. She pressed her hips provocatively against the front of his jeans. He was twanging, all right, she gloated. Throbbing too. The only trouble was, so was she.

Under the guise of getting a better view of the mountains, she moved out of contact with him.

"Where did you say that mountain was?" She couldn't have seen it if she had walked into it nose first.

"Over there." His arm rested on her shoulder as he pointed.

"Ahhh, yes."

They stood that way for a while, blindly viewing a mountain while their nerves screamed and their minds beat against the restraints they had set.

Rick cleared his throat.

Martha Ann coughed.

"Well . . ." he said.

"Yes?" She was so glad for a break in the tension, she forgot where she was standing. She turned quickly and found herself practically in his arms.

For a moment they both stood looking at each other, paralyzed.

If I kiss her now, I am lost, he thought.

If he touches me now, I can't be responsible, she thought.

He stepped backward. "I should be going."

"Oh."

"To take a bath."

"Of course." She flicked her tongue over her dry lips.

He made a strangled sound. He had to get out of that bedroom. Fast. Never breaking stride, he called to her over his shoulder. "I'll bathe and change and pick you up in about an hour. Then we'll go and find your husband."

The door banged shut behind him.

She groped her way to the bed and collapsed. Her heart was still beating so hard, she could hear the blood pounding in her ears. Good heavens. She had almost wound up giving herself to a man who owned whorehouses. She pressed her hand to her forehead and groaned. That just proved that she didn't have a lick of sense about men. Goodness gracious. Was Lucky O'Grady worth all this?

She lay back against the pillows for a while, letting her breathing come back to normal. What she needed was a good stiffening of her resolve.

She picked up the phone and dialed her sister.

"Evelyn? Is that you?"

"Of course, it's me. Is that you, Martha Ann? You sound funny."

"It's these tight clothes. I can hardly breathe."

"What tight clothes? You're not making one bit of sense. Martha Ann, what are you up to now?"

"I'm here in Las Vegas. We're going to look for Lucky."

"I *know* that. You didn't have to waste a long-distance phone call just to tell me that. Do you know how much these prime-time rates are? Good heavens, Martha Ann! I'll bet you could buy lunch for what this call is costing. Why—"

"Evelyn!"

"What?"

"I'm in terrible trouble."

"Oh, no!" There was deathly silence on the line as the Riley sisters tried to read each other's minds.

"It's not what you're thinking, Evelyn."

"How do you know what I'm thinking?"

"I always do. You're thinking I've lost my purse again."

"Have you?"

"Goodness no. I've just about lost your virginity."

Evelyn laughed. "I lost that a long time ago—to Lucky."

"Well, your reputation then. Evelyn, I think I'm falling in love with Rick McGill."

"You call that terrible trouble! Why, good heavens, Martha Ann, I call that good news."

"He's a scoundrel."

"He's handsome."

"He owns bordellos."

"Somebody has to."

"What am I going to do?"

"Just listen to your heart. I always did. . . . And Martha Ann . . ."

"What?"

"In spite of the way things have turned out, I've never regretted it."

By the time Rick knocked on her door, Martha Ann was as scrubbed and decent as she could make herself in the risqué costume. She had washed the bright red lipstick off her face and lips, and she had closed the zipper so that no thigh was showing except below the bottom of the skirt. She had also strengthened her resolve. Evelyn needed her. No matter what it took, she would go out there and find Lucky.

Rick noticed her toned-down look. Although he had never believed for a minute that she really had liked the sleazy outfit, he was glad to see changes. They helped ease his conscience over buying the ridiculous costume in the first place.

"Ready to go?" he asked.

"Lead me to the tables."

"Do you think that's where he'll be?"

"I *know* that's where he'll be. If there's a big game going on, Lucky will be right in the middle of it."

The elevator whisked them downstairs to the casino. It was decorated with purple carpet, pink marble columns, a life-size statue of Elvis, and as many chandeliers as there was space on the ceiling. Las Vegas's idea of elegance, Martha Ann thought. Still, the gaudy scene tugged at her. She had grown up near Vegas, had spent many hours in front of the felt-covered tables. Her future had once hinged on the roll of the dice. She felt a familiar surge of adrenaline, a clamoring of excitement, an itch to try her luck.

"Do you gamble?" she asked Rick.

"Yes. But not with money."

"Oh."

"Why don't we walk around the casino and see if we can spot Lucky?"

"We'll be less conspicuous if we play."

"Fine. I have nothing against a game or two."

They walked to the roulette wheel, and Rick plunked down a dollar. One spin of the wheel, and his dollar was scooped up and added to the hotel's treasury. He lost four more in quick succession.

"I don't seem to have the touch."

"A spin of the wheel is a quick way to lose money."

Rick glanced around the casino. The sounds of gambling were all around him—the clink of money against the slot machines, the occasional buzzing when one of the machines gave up a small portion of its wealth, the calling of the croupiers, the excited high-pitched chatter of the gamblers.

"It seems to me that all of it is a quick way to lose money." He took her elbow and steered her away from the roulette wheel. "Maybe I'll have better luck with keno."

"Ugh."

"Was that a comment on the game or on my skills?" Rick grinned.

"Keno is too tame for me."

One eyebrow arched upward. "You play?"

"Some."

"Mrs. O'Grady, you never cease to amaze me."

"You have to remember that I had a little exposure to gambling when I was growing up."

"Just what every growing girl needs." He chuckled with appreciation. "Tell me, Mrs. O'Grady, if you had a stake—say one hundred dollars—what would you do with it?"

"Turn it into a fortune. Anyway if I hit a winning streak, Lucky might come to us. He never could. resist a hot game."

"This I gotta see." He peeled off five twenties and handed them to her.

"You can add it to my tab."

"I'm willing to gamble. If you lose it, I'll put it on your tab. If you win, I'll call it even."

"What will you get out of that deal?"

"Pleasure, my dear. Pure pleasure. And that's a bargain at any price."

He led her to a table where a large crowd of people were cheering on a tall man in a Stetson and cowboy boots. With every roll of the dice, he came up a winner. His spirits were high, his money pile was growing, and his shooting hand was hot.

Martha Ann Riley took him on. She sidled up to the table as cool as you please, never batting an eyelash at the stares she got in her outrageously provocative outfit. The lady was pure class, Rick decided. His conscience hurt him over the outfit. Tomorrow he'd make amends.

At first Rick got in the game himself. He wasn't a

gambler, but he didn't mind losing twenty or so if he was having fun. He called it entertainment.

Soon, though, he pulled out to watch Martha Ann. She was good—better than good—she had the touch. Her stack of winnings grew higher and higher. She was fun to watch and fun to be with. Her exuberance seemed to infect the whole table.

"Roll 'em, lady," they yelled.

"Atta girl."

"Break the bank!"

"*Heeere* she goes. Hot dang!"

By the time she pulled out, she was flushed and laughing.

"Let's cash in," she said.

"You're still winning."

"I always quit while I'm ahead."

"Smart lady." He fingered the chips she had handed him. "How much do you think we won?"

"We?"

His smile was devilish as he looked at her. "You couldn't have done it without me, sweetheart. I was your head cheerleader."

"If you're going to be my cheerleader, we need to get you some new clothes—tights and a tank top and a couple of pom-poms."

"I draw the line at tights, but I'll show you my pom-poms if you like."

She punched his arm. "You're terrible."

"I try. I try."

The easy friendship took them both by surprise. Somehow she had forgotten her role as pregnant wife and he had abandoned all pretense of being a rogue. It felt good to both of them.

"Do you know something? You're not as bad as you make yourself out to be, Rick McGill."

"Tell me more. I love to be fawned over."

"I don't fawn, but I'm not above giving a little compliment now and then."

"Go to it, sweetheart. I want my head to get big enough to wear one of those Stetsons."

She laughed. "You'd look awful in a Stetson. You're not the type."

"What type am I?"

"My sister says you're a blond Clark Gable."

"You have a sister?" He knew good and well she had a sister. He merely wanted to hear the truth from her. Though why the truth was important, he couldn't say. Nor did he want to know.

"Yes." Careful, she told herself. She was supposed to *be* her sister. In a manner of speaking. She put her hand on her forehead to see if she was coming down with an attack of something disastrous. Something called I-can't-lie-to-this-man-anymore. "Her name is Evelyn." She watched his face to see how he took that news.

"Nice name," he said without a flicker of emotion.

Good, she thought. She'd told the truth, and nothing terrible had happened.

Rick handed their bundle of chips to the cashier on the other side of the window and turned back to Martha Ann. "Is your sister married too?"

"Yes. As a matter of fact she is."

"What's her name?"

"I already told you—Evelyn."

"I meant her married name."

He handed her a big wad of bills, and she could swear there was a devilish twinkle in his eye. As a matter of fact, he looked like a big cat toying with a mouse. How much did this man really know, she wondered. After all, he was a private eye. The best according to rumor. What was to prevent him from checking up on the Riley girls? Oh, help. Had this

rogue, this unscrupulous keeper of bordellos know
all along that she wasn't married to Lucky O'Grady
If so, then he wasn't a wife-chaser after all. Of course
there was still his ill-gotten wealth.

The money rustled in her hand as she folded the
crisp new bills. Who was she to talk? she though
wryly. Here she was holding a handful of gambling
winnings and condemning Rick McGill for his money
making methods. Good grief, was she turning into a
prude?

"Martha Ann?"

"What?" Her head jerked up, and she found him
staring at her in a most disconcerting way.

"I asked you what your sister's married name is."

There was nothing she could do except go on
pretending.

"Her husband's name is . . . Charles Madison
Mitchum . . . the third."

"Hmmmm. I know some Mitchums from Tupelo
Is he—"

"He's not from around there. His family is from
. . . New York. They're in the . . . import-export busi
ness. James is out of town a lot."

"I thought you said his name was Charles."

"It is. James Charles." Oh, help. What had she
said.

He was grinning like a possum at a picnic.

"Look, this isn't helping to find my own husband."

"Ah, yes. Lucky. Why don't we walk down the
Strip and check the other casinos?" He took her
elbow, and they wound their way past the gaming
tables and the milling mob of tourists toward the
revolving front doors. "By the way, Martha Ann
does Lucky know he's going to be a father?"

"Well . . . no. I barely know I'm going to be a
mother."

Rick grinned. "Is that so? Just found out, did you?"

She waved her hand airily. "Of course I suspected it. Women know these things almost instinctively. But I didn't *really* know it until . . . that day in the creek."

He reached down and patted her stomach. "I'd say that baby knows how to make an entrance."

"Michael's a smart kid." She grinned. It didn't seem to matter what sort of crazy carrying-on Rick McGill was doing, she always found his company to be exciting, stimulating, and altogether wonderful. She sighed. She supposed she was one of those women who were destined to fall in love with a man, not because of what he was but *in spite of* what he was.

They walked together down the street. Blazing neon signs cast red, blue, yellow, and green shadows over their skin. Rick reached down and caught her hand. He didn't hold it captive like a fragile and unwilling bird: He linked his fingers through hers in a simple let's-be-friends fashion that was totally endearing.

Holding hands. That's what love was all about, she thought. She was so happy, she forgot to look for Lucky.

Eight

They didn't go back to their hotel until three A.M. Standing in front of Martha Ann's door, Rick gazed down at her. He didn't know why he wasn't scheming for ways to get into her room and into her bed. But he wasn't. All he was feeling at the moment was tender concern for a woman who was looking for her sister's husband, a woman who was sweet and funny and fiesty and exciting and breathlessly passionate.

He tipped her chin up with one finger and looked into her eyes.

"We'll find Lucky, sweetheart."

"I know we will. Tonight is just the beginning."

The words sounded prophetic to him. He guessed he must be getting dotty in his old age. What's more, calling her 'sweetheart' was no longer a calculated imitation of movie bad boy Humphrey Bogart. By george, when he'd said it this time, he had *really* meant it.

"That's right. Just the beginning."

How could a man resist those blue eyes, he thought. He slid his hand down her throat and across her shoulder. With gentle pressure he pulled her closer. She settled her head on his shoulder as if it belonged there. And perhaps it did. He didn't know anymore.

"A hug for luck," he said.

Her laughter was muffled against his neck. "Or is that a hug for Lucky?"

He tightened his hold. Lord, this woman could cuddle better than anybody else in the world. He squeezed her just a little tighter.

"How about a hug just between friends?" His voice had gotten husky, and he knew that if he didn't pull away, a hug wouldn't suffice.

"Sounds good to me."

They swayed together a while, enjoying the closeness of two naturally affectionate people who understood the joys of touching.

Finally Rick spoke. "I'm sorry about the clothes, Martha Ann. I'll get you some decent ones tomorrow."

"It doesn't matter. These suit the occasion quite well." She chuckled again, and her warm breath sent shivers skittering over his skin. "Actually, I'm foolishly flattered that an old girl like me can still look halfway decent in a costume this daring."

Rick hugged her even closer, then stepped back. "Do you mind if an old boy like me tells an old girl like you what fun tonight has been?"

"You've made it so."

The long look they exchanged was full of a thousand unspoken feelings. Even without touching they seemed to be melting into each other. Finally Rick shook his head like an old dog coming out of anesthesia.

"Good night, Martha Ann."

"Good night, Rick."

"See you in the morning."

Her hand shook as she fitted her key into the lock. She bit her lower lip and forced herself to calm down. Finally the key went in, and she opened the door. Inside her cool dark room she leaned against the doorjamb. She felt limp. What Rick McGill hadn't been able to accomplish in several days of torrid kisses and steamy seduction, he had been able to do in the space of a few hours simply by holding her hand and hugging her.

She was dreadfully, irrationally, irreversibly in love with a scoundrel. The thought made her groan aloud. Of course, she'd done nothing but lie to him from the moment they had met. There was no way a man could ever trust a lying woman, let alone fall in love with her. Her web of lies had saved her. Or had they trapped her? She was too confused to know anything right now.

She undressed and went to bed, but she didn't have high hopes that her personal plight would look much better in the morning.

Rick and Martha Ann spent the next two days searching religiously for Lucky O'Grady. They haunted the gambling casinos and the smoky nightclubs. But all they accomplished was parlaying Martha Ann's hundred-dollar stake into an impressive figure—$4,198.50.

On the third day they decided to take a break.

They bought picnic supplies, rented a car, and set out for the mountains.

"There's a wonderful cave in these mountains," Martha Ann told Rick as they drove along. "It's called Crystal Cave by ordinary folks, but the Indians used to call it the Magic Music Cave."

"Why was it called that?"

"One of the legends had it that the Indians could go there to hear the music of their spirits."

"Search for identity?"

"Precisely."

The car they had rented was a convertible. Rick propped his left arm on the door, enjoying the feel of the hot sun on his skin. They were going at a sedate pace, the better to enjoy the view, but still the wind ruffled their hair and whistled around their ears. He glanced at his passenger. Dressed in her own clothes, wearing little makeup that he could tell, she looked like a breathless view of the sunrise at daybreak.

He laughed with the sheer exuberance of living. Shoot, he thought. By the time he got back to Tupelo, he'd be in such a poetic mood, he'd have to sit down and write a song—or a book of poetry. Or heck, why not even a whole love story? Everybody else was doing it.

He wondered if Martha Ann was feeling as mellow as he was.

"A penny for your thoughts, sweetheart."

She turned toward Rick and propped her arm along the top of the seat. Her fingertips brushed his shoulder. She let her hand rest there on his sunwarmed skin. That just went to show the progress in their relationship since they had come to Las Vegas, he thought.

"I was wondering if we'd hear the music of our souls in the Magic Music Cave."

"I'm afraid mine would be out of tune. I don't have an ear for harmony. The only song I can sing is 'Boogie Woogie Bugle Boy' and not very well." He demonstrated.

She laughed. She'd never hear that song again without thinking of the man she loved—and had deceived. She couldn't forget that, she reminded herself. It was best to play out her role until she was safely back in Tupelo with her sister's husband in tow.

"Don't you ever take anything seriously?" she asked.

"I do. The flag, motherhood, and popcorn."

"I thought that was apple pie."

"Don't tell anybody, but I'm one of the few people in America who can't stand the sight of apple pie. It all comes from stealing little green apples once and getting so sick, even my mother thought I was going to die."

"Is your mother living?"

"She's not only living, she's kicking up her heels. She and Dad are both seventy-three, and right now they are on a big game safari."

"They're hunting animals?"

"With cameras."

"What a relief."

He thought that was a strange remark coming from a woman who lately had made a career of lying and who probably never intended to see him again once they got back to Tupelo. Why should she care if his family were horse thieves? Still . . . he glanced her way again. He was glad she was relieved about his family.

"My sister Jo Beth is a photojournalist. We consider her the wild one in the family," he said. "She's with Mom and Dad."

"Any brothers?"

"Danny, the oldest, is a doctor. He's married now and has three of the sweetest little girls you'll ever see. Andrew, the youngest, would make you wash your mouth out with soap if you even mentioned marriage. He and I are a lot alike—confirmed bachelors."

She looked at his profile. Why did that statement

give her a sinking feeling right in the pit of her stomach? Best not to think too much about it. She turned her attention back to the scenery.

They arrived at Crystal Cave right at lunchtime. Rick uncorked the bottle of wine, while Martha Ann unwrapped the sandwiches. After lunch they stowed their picnic leftovers and went inside the cave.

It was beautiful in an eerie, haunting sort of way. Huge gypsum formations rose from the floor and hung from the ceiling. Even in the darkness of the cave, the crystals sparkled. Their glow created a special atmosphere that the Indians surely would have thought to be magic. Rick seemed to be feeling that magic himself. If he weren't careful, he'd soon be hearing the music too.

He and Martha Ann meandered along behind a small group of tourists who were spending more time listening to their guide than looking at the beauty and wonder around them.

The tour guide was a tall raw-boned woman with a severe hairdo and a stern voice. "The Indians thought there was music in this cave," she said. "Naturally it was only the wind blowing."

Rick leaned down and whispered to Martha Ann. "I like your version better."

"So do I." As a matter of fact, she was hearing some of that music herself. Or maybe she was just feeling mellow from too much wine. In any case, she wanted Rick all to herself in this magical setting. She smiled up at him. "Do you mind being adventurous?"

"I like adventure next to the best."

"Next to what?"

"Making love."

A sudden vision of Velma's curtained bed came to Martha Ann. How close she had come to indulging in Rick's favorite pastime! As she led him away from the tour group and through a series of passageways that she remembered from her childhood, she knew with absolute clarity that making love with Rick McGill would never be a casual thing. She guessed she'd known it all along, since that day she'd first laid eyes on him. Oh, heavens. Not only was she addicted to the wrong kind of man, she was hopelessly romantic. Love at first sight. Good grief. She must be a throwback to the forties.

"Where are we going?"

"There's a special place I know, faraway from the maddening crowd."

He seemed pleased by her answer. Their hands were linked, and he swung hers jauntily, like a schoolboy with his favorite sweetheart. "I guess you have designs on me, huh?"

She gave him a frank perusal. "Any woman in her right mind would—that is, except a pregnant one."

"Married to boot."

"That too."

They were deep in the heart of the cave now. The formations were bigger and richer, with a deeper, more mysterious glow. The air was colder and heavier, and it seemed to pulse with a strange sort of music. Rick sneaked a peek at Martha Ann, and a strange revelation came to him: She was the music that stirred his soul. It was as clear to him as one of the shining crystal formations. Whatever he had told himself about making her a playmate, whatever he had planned about staying footloose and fancy-free until he was fifty didn't apply anymore. Not with this woman. Not with Martha Ann Riley. She was some kind of special, and he guessed that scared him just a little bit. His parents' marriage was perfect. So was his brother's. It would be hard if not downright impossible to live up to that kind of family tradition. Of course, he'd never considered himself a coward. Still, he wasn't ready to admit that he was hearing the music of love. Anyhow, love didn't sneak up on a man; it was that great big neon sign that lit up the sky, and he hadn't seen one with his name on it yet.

Martha Ann stopped walking when they were outside a tiny opening.

"How do you feel about crawling?" she asked.

"As long as you don't ask me to grovel."

"Right through there is one of the most beautiful spots in the world."

"I'm game. Who goes first?"

"I will since I know the place."

She got down on all fours and crept through the opening, then she turned to help him squeeze through.

"Are you stuck?"

"No . . . but if you could just give me a little tug . . . ouch, careful of my pom-poms. I'm partial to cheerleading."

She tugged his shoulders, and he popped into the secret place with the suddenness of a champagne cork leaving a bottle. When he had righted himself and was seated beside Martha Ann, he looked at his surroundings. She had been right about the place. It was a small, private chamber where crystal literally lined the walls. The formations on the ceiling looked like shimmering lace curtains, and running through the middle of the room was an icy blue stream of sparkling water.

"If a man can't hear the music of his soul here, he's deaf." The sound of his voice echoed around the crystal chamber.

"Let's walk down closer to the stream."

Taking Rick's hand seemed the natural thing to do. She took it without a thought. Even their footsteps sounded musical as they walked toward the stream.

"Careful. There's a slippery spot." Rick put his arm around Martha Ann's waist to steady her.

"I'm steady on my feet. There's no way I can fall."

"Just in case." He kept his arm there.

She turned her head, tilting it back ever so slightly, and looked at him. What she saw made her catch her breath. All the magic of the cave was shining in his eyes. She lifted her right hand as if to ward off what she saw. He took it and drew her into his arms.

He kissed her. There in the crystal cave with the music of their souls swirling around them they didn't need preliminaries. They didn't need words.

His lips savored hers with a pent-up hunger that took them both by surprise. Three days in Vegas searching for Lucky with an easy camaraderie had not put out the blaze they'd ignited that first night in the Valley of Fire. If anything, the waiting only made this moment sweeter, more precious.

Martha Ann pressed closer to him, molding her body down the muscular length of his. Something wonderful was happening. She knew it, and she sensed that he knew it too. Why fight it any longer? Her head tilted backward, and her mouth received his questing tongue. The delicious warm friction inside her mouth melted her bones. She dug her fingernails into his back.

He cupped her hips and pulled them tightly against his own. It was an invitation she couldn't resist.

"Ahh, Rick." She tugged his shirt out of the waistband of his jeans and slid her hands over his back. He shuddered.

"My fiery . . . funny . . . sweetheart." The words were murmured against her lips as his hands worked on the buttons of her blouse.

He lifted his head and gazed down at her. "You are exceptionally beautiful." His hands divided the front of her blouse and slowly peeled it back. "Exquisite." Out of necessity, she was wearing the bra he had purchased, the bawdy, made-for-seduction bra that bared her nipples. They were tight with desire. He bent down and took one into his mouth while his hands slid the blouse slowly down her shoulders.

A slow burning heat spread through her. She gripped his shoulders and pulled him closer. Ahhh, saints preserve her, his mouth felt like heaven. She couldn't stop now if she wanted to. And she didn't want to.

They were both making sounds of pleasure now, unintelligible sounds known only to lovers. Slowly he turned her in his arms so that her back was pressed firmly against him. She could feel the size and heat of him through their jeans.

"Lean . . . on . . . me . . . sweetheart," he murmured hoarsely against her neck. She let her head go limp on his shoulder. "That's . . . a . . . pet."

His left hand toyed with her nipples, and his right slid smoothly into the waistband of her jeans. He spread his flattened palm over her stomach. She sucked in her breath. His touch, she thought. His touch was driving her wild.

His hand dipped lower, and his fingers deftly pushed aside her silk panties. It had gone beyond kissing, but she knew she couldn't turn back. When his fingers began to stroke her, she could do nothing except give in to the sweet, hot sensations that curled upward and turned her into putty.

She moved her head and blindly pressed her lips against the side of his throat. She had to feel his flesh under her mouth. What he was doing to her was driving her mad, insane, totally crazy in a wild and wanton way.

When his index finger entered her, she involuntarily thrust her hips forward.

"That's . . . it, . . . sweetheart. Go . . . with . . . it." His voice was hoarse, and his breathing was ragged.

The music of the cave whispered around them, and the music of their souls drove them on. The rhythm of his erotic stroking increased. She moved with it. Time was suspended. Nothing existed except the wild sensations that swept through them.

Her breath climbed high in her throat until she thought she wasn't going to be able to breathe. Perspiration gathered on her brow and trickled between her breasts. She needed . . . she wanted . . . release. When it came, it was an explosion that left her damp and limp.

Her head lolled on his shoulder, and she moaned. He turned her slowly in his arms and took her lips. With exquisite tenderness, he brought her back into the realm of control.

"Ahhh, sweetheart." He brushed his lips against hers again. "What you do to me."

"Hmmm." It was all she could manage at the moment. She had a feeling that she would have sunk to the floor if his hand hadn't been supporting her back.

His hands cupped her cheeks. "Tonight, my pet . . ." He paused long enough to press kisses all over her face. ". . . when we are safe in the privacy of my room . . ." He paused again to bend down and kiss her nipple. ". . . we'll finish what we started."

Oh, no, she thought. What had she started? She leaned her head against his shoulder, giving herself time to think. He hadn't said one word about love. As far as she knew, he was still a confirmed rake bent on seduction. Love. Why didn't he say the word? If he had, she would have tossed aside her charade and bared her soul. She groaned, partly in agony and partly in ecstasy.

"I take it that's a yes, sweetheart."

Nothing had changed, she thought. Nothing *could* change.

"No." Still damp and limp, she stepped back from him.

"Did you say no?" He couldn't believe what he was hearing. In the last three days he'd shown his care and consideration for Martha Ann in every way he knew possible. He'd abandoned all the games, all the pretense. And just now, in this beautiful crystal chamber, he had unselfishly given her pleasure. Didn't she have one bit of feeling for him?

"I said no." She bent over and picked up her blouse. "Good grief. Are you forgetting? I'm a married woman. A married pregnant woman."

She was going to drive him to cuss, he thought. That's all there was to it. What would it take to make her give up that fool lying game she was playing? Professions of love? By george, he wasn't about to make a fool of himself with a woman who apparently didn't give one whit about him. If she did care, she wouldn't keep on lying.

He was still tightly wound with his own need. Her quick dismissal didn't improve his temper one bit.

"Allow me to help you with your blouse, *Mrs. O'Grady*. After all, I'm the one who took it off." He jerked the blouse shut and began to fasten the buttons, taking great care to fondle and play with her as much as possible. He wanted to drive her as crazy as she was driving him.

He succeeded.

The quick burst of sweet, hot moisture between her thighs let her know in plain terms that she wanted Rick McGill and everything he had to offer. She wanted him so much, she had to clench her jaw to keep from voicing her need. She still didn't know whether he *knew* she wasn't married or whether he *thought* she was. And she wasn't going to find out. There was no way on earth she would become the playmate of another heartbreaking, two-timing, wife-chasing man.

"If you're all finished now, we'll leave." She spoke between clenched teeth.

"I'm not finished yet, Mrs. O'Grady. Not by a long shot."

He swept her into his arms, bent her over backward in the manner of Rudolph Valentino seducing a silent screen star, and kissed her savagely. There was no tenderness, no love, no sweetness in the kiss. It was pure wild and fierce revenge.

"Show me how much you mean that no." His mouth ground into hers again, and he held her so tightly, she could barely breathe. "Show me."

She was seduced by him all over again. It didn't seem to matter whether he was fierce and wild, sweet and tender, or mocking and funny, she wanted Rick McGill. His hips plunged against hers in a frantic imitation of love, and she responded with a wantonness that belied her words.

Heaven help her, she thought, for she couldn't seem to help herself.

When he finally released her, she was puffy-lipped

nd weak-kneed. It was a terrible state for Mrs. Lucky
)'Grady to be in. After they found Lucky, she'd *have*
o tell Rick the truth. Otherwise her sister's reputa-
ion would be in ruin.

"Let's go," she said. She was glad to have the
xcuse to get down on her hands and knees and
rawl for she didn't think her legs would hold her up
nuch longer. She gulped big mouthfuls of air as
he slowly negotiated her way through the narrow
•pening.

Behind her, Rick patted her bottom. "Take your
ime, sweetheart. The view back here is great."

She made a choked sound that passed for protest.
It the moment, she was beyond caring whether he
inderstood or not.

They rode back to the hotel in total, icy silence.
They didn't even comment on the magnificent sunset. What did it matter that the mountains around
he city were putting on a display of royal colors
vorthy of a king? Neither of them cared. All that
nattered was the rift between them. The camarade-
ie of the last three days was hopelessly lost. So was
he exhilarating give-and-take of their cat-and-mouse
:ourtship.

Rick was bound and determined not to give an
nch, and so was she. By the time they had parked
it the hotel and reached the elevators, they were
)oth so stiff-lipped and rigid, they looked like two
·obots.

When the elevator deposited them on their floor,
hey still didn't speak. Halfway down the hall a fat
voman with frizzy brown hair rose from her spot in
ront of Martha Ann's door. She was holding the
1and of a blushing, giggling skinny girl who looked

about sixteen but who had the kind of face that could belong to a woman of any age.

"Excuse me," the fat woman said.

Martha Ann was so wrapped up in her own problems that she jumped.

"I didn't mean to scare you." The woman put out her hand and briefly touched Martha Ann's arm.

Rick was immediately on the alert. He gave the woman a look that caused her to release Martha Ann's arm and step back.

"I don't mean no harm. Honest." She spread her hands wide. "I'm just a maid here at the hotel, see, and I wanted to talk to you. It's about Lurlene here." She put her hand in the small of the girl's back and pushed her forward.

"If you need help, I'm sure there are services in the city for that. I can do some phoning for you," Rick said.

The fat woman laughed. "It ain't phoning I want, it's another one of them little mesh bags."

"What little mesh bags?" Rick gave Martha Ann a quizzical look.

The fat lady appealed to Martha Ann. "You was the one that throwed it out, wadn't you?"

"Are you talking about the bag I put in the waste-basket a few days ago?"

"Yep. That's the one." She heaved herself up straight, sucked in her breath, and patted her hair. "I knew what it was the minute I saw it. Had a friend once—her name was Sara Light Foot. She used to make them things all the time. You oughta seen the miracles she done. Why, them little bags could turn a icicle into a bonfire."

"What was in the bag?" Rick asked.

The fat woman burst out laughing. "Oh, lordy

mister. It wadn't what was in 'em that was important, it's what they done. Why, I took that bag home
and hung it over my bed, and my old man hasn't let
me git a minute's rest since." She chuckled again.
"A love potion. That's what it was."

"Love potion?" Rick and Martha Ann spoke at the
same time and turned to look at each other.

"One of the Running Bears put it in the bag Velma
packed for me," Martha Ann explained to Rick. "I
found it the day we checked in."

"You mean that smelly little thing was a love potion? I guess that explains things, huh?" Rick gave
her a wry grin.

"It had to be the love potion, because it certainly
wasn't due to any feelings on my part." She spoke
out of anger, for she was still stung by his refusal to
admit any feelings for her except lust.

"Nor on mine."

They could probably have stared at each other
indefinitely if the fat woman hadn't interrupted
them.

"You never did say if you had any more of them
things. You see, Lurlene here is gettin' married, and
that Wayne is kinda shy and backward in some
things. They need a love potion mighty bad."

"I'm sorry. There are no more love potions." Martha Ann was still gazing at Rick as she spoke.

"I'm sorry too." His voice had softened. It sounded
almost as if he were making an apology to Martha
Ann. Naturally she decided she was foolish to think
such a thing. That's what happened to women in
love, they lost their common sense.

She shook her head and forced herself to look
away from Rick. "Perhaps your friend Sara Light
Foot could make one for you."

"Lordy, I'd a gone to her in the first place, if she was still around here. She lit out three years ago with one of them electric evangelists."

"Electric evangelist?" Martha Ann stifled her giggle.

"You know, one of them TV preachers." She smoothed her wrinkled dress over her fat hips and took Lurlene's arm. "Well, honey, we might as well be gettin' on. I guess I can let you borrow the potion— but just for a few days." She laughed self-consciously. "Lordy, lordy, I wouldn't want to do without it for no longer than that." Tugging Lurlene along, she started down the hallway, then turned back for one last word. "You two musta been through with it, or you wouldn't never have throwed it out."

"We were finished with it," Martha Ann said.

"Yes. Absolutely."

Rick's quick agreement stung Martha Ann. She turned her back to him and fitted her key in the lock.

"Martha Ann . . ."

She whirled around, a half-smile of expectation on her face. "What?"

"I'm going out to look for your husband. Alone. I'm ready to find him and get out of this place."

"That suits me perfectly. The sooner we leave here the better."

She shoved open her door and waited a second for him to say something, anything to breach the terrible rift between them. He didn't, and she slammed the door with a satisfying, wall-rattling bang.

Rick spun around and strode down the hall. He had never met such an all-fired, stubborn woman in his life. He decided it was a good thing he hadn't made a fool of himself in the cave and made some stupid declaration of undying affection. Shoot, he was lucky he hadn't seen that great neon sign in the sky. Love. Who needed it?

He punched the elevator button viciously. Somewhere out there was Lucky O'Grady, and Rick was going to find him if he had to call in the police, the National Guard, and the FBI. He needed to get away from Las Vegas and back home where he could find a sweet, willing playmate to take his mind off the conniving Martha Ann Riley.

A sudden vision of that beauty spot beside her lips came to him. By george, she was going to be a hard woman to get off his mind.

At six o'clock the next morning Rick returned to the hotel with Lucky O'Grady in tow. The sheepish-looking captive was rumpled, bleary-eyed, and penitent.

"Hey, man, I didn't mean to put anybody to all this trouble," Lucky was saying as he and Rick stepped off the elevator. "Evelyn knows I have to have a little space every now and then. It's not like her to send somebody after me."

Rick was in no mood to be nice. "Maybe she had her reasons."

"I wonder what they could be."

"You left a pregnant wife to run off and gamble, and you don't know what her reasons are for trying to find you? Don't give me that innocent good-old-boy routine. You're too intelligent for that."

Lucky pushed a shaky hand through his tousled dark hair. "Hell, yeah. I know it. I just keep making excuses for myself."

"Don't you think it's about time you quit making excuses and started accepting your responsibilities?" Who was he to talk, the little voice of Rick's conscience asked him. A man who wanted to play around till he was fifty? He ignored the smart-mouthed little fellow. He'd been up all night; he figured he deserved to let off steam by lecturing Lucky O'Grady.

"You don't know how many times I've asked myself that same question. I keep promising my wife I'm going to do better. Lord knows, she deserves better. I swear, this time I'm going to change."

"Don't swear it to me. Tell her."

"She's here?"

"Right behind that door." Rick figured the devil made him say that. Or perhaps it was revenge. In any case, posing as Lucky's wife had been Martha Ann's idea. He'd let her handle it.

He rapped on her door.

"Who is it?" Her voice sounded sleepy. Good. He was glad he'd awakened her. He hadn't slept a wink and might never get another good night's sleep as long as he lived. Why should she?

"Open up, sweetheart. I've found your husband."

"Lucky?" Her voice sounded perkier now, though it was somewhat muffled and he couldn't be sure. There was a long silence and then she flung open the door. By george, that woman looked delicious in her morning dishabille. Rick reached out and patted her cheek. He couldn't seem to resist touching her. "It's all over, sweetheart. I'm delivering your lover straight to your arms." Having said all that, he stepped back and revealed Lucky O'Grady.

Lucky's mouth fell open. "Martha Ann?"

She pulled him into the room, flung her arms around him, and whispered, "Don't you *dare* mess this up." Then she leaned back and assumed a wifely look of concern. "Darling, where have you been? We've been looking everywhere for you."

"Well, you can stop looking now. I'm here." He pushed her aside and headed toward the bed. "I'm tired as a dog. Do you mind if I take a nap?" He stretched out on the bed and shut his eyes.

Rick was leaning against the doorjamb, watching the entire scene. He didn't know whether to be amused or mad. *It's over now,* he wanted to shout. *Tell me the truth, Martha Ann.*

But she didn't. She continued her charade.

"Thank you *so* much for finding my husband. As soon as I get back home, I'll pay you." She gazed toward the bed with feigned affection. "Poor baby, he's all tuckered out." Lucky was already snoring.

"I always expect immediate payment." Rick stepped into the room and quietly shut the door. Lucky kept snoring.

"As you well know, I lost everything in the crash."

"Not everything."

Seeing the gleam in Rick's eyes, Martha Ann backed behind a chair. He stalked her.

"Do you think a little thing like that chair is going to stop me?" He lifted it and set it aside.

"You forget yourself. My husband is on the bed."

Rick caught her shoulders and tipped her chin up with one finger. "If *I* were your husband, sweetheart, you'd be on that bed with me."

"Let me go, you . . ." Words failed her.

"What, my pet? Scoundrel? Blackguard? Rake? Come on, my sweet. Don't stop now." His hand tightened on her chin. "You've called me everything but liar. Is that the word you're looking for?" He wanted the truth from her. Standing there with his hands on her face, he suddenly realized how much he wanted to hear her tell the truth. *Don't you have any trust in me?* he wanted to shout. "Is it, sweetheart?" His voice was soft and silky in a deadly sort of way.

"No." Her shoulders sagged. "You're all those things I called you, but as far as I know, you've never lied to me."

He felt a twinge of conscience. If playing a role qualified as lying, he was guilty. His face softened.

"About that payment, sweetheart . . ." He pulled her swiftly into his arms and crushed her protest with his mouth. The kiss was hungry, savage, punishing. He didn't know what he sought to prove, or even if he was trying to prove anything. All he knew was that he had to have her one more time. He had to feel those luscious lips under his.

Hers parted, and she kissed him back with careless abandon. She wound her arms around his neck and pulled him fiercely to her. Afterward she might never see him again, she thought. Fate was saving her from another mistake, but that didn't make her feel a darned bit better. Unshed tears were making her eyes sting. But she'd be darned if she'd cry for Rick McGill. After all, playmates weren't supposed to cry.

His mouth left hers and roamed down the side of her throat. "All that fire, my pet . . ." He undid the two top buttons on her blouse and bent his head over her breasts. "No bra. I approve."

She groaned. The loud snoring from the bed seemed to mock her. She knew she was playing with fire, but she was beyond caring.

Rick dragged her hips tightly against his. She sucked in her breath. There was no doubt what was motivating him. Desire. Pure and simple.

He teased her nipples with his teeth and tongue. A slow heat built in the center of her body and radiated outward.

"Oh, nooo," she said on a moan.

"Oh, yes, my pet. Oh, yes." He lifted his head and took her lips again.

Love had turned her into a crazy woman, she decided. Her brother-in-law was sleeping on the bed, and she didn't care if Rick lowered her to the carpet then and there and made love.

When she thought she was going to pull him down to the floor herself, he lifted his head. Not far. Just a fraction of an inch from her lips.

"Does your husband know that he got cheated?"

"Cheated?" With her blood boiling and racing in her veins and her carrying on like some demented fool, she hardly knew what she was saying.

"You greeted him more like a sister than a torrid, hungry wife." He gripped her chin and forced her to look into his eyes. "Does he know you save all your kisses for me?"

She tried to jerk away, but he held her firm.

"You've had your so-called *payment*. What more do you want?"

The truth, his mind screamed. But he had too much pride to say so. If she ever told him the truth, she had to do it voluntarily. He waited a while longer, begging her, compelling her with his eyes to confide in him. When it became clear to him that she wasn't going to say anything, he let her go.

Stepping back, he ran his hand over his stubbly chin. "A little amusement, sweetheart. That's all I want."

"That's what I thought." She cupped her face with her hands. Her lips felt swollen, and her chin stung. Beard burn. Rick McGill was determined to leave his mark on her, one way or the other.

"You've been very entertaining, Mrs. O'Grady. Perhaps next time we'll have the ultimate fun."

"There won't be a next time."

"There'll always be a next time for us, sweetheart."

"So you've said."

"And so you've proven." He turned and strode across the room. When he reached the door, he turned back around. "Your tickets home will be at the front desk." He glanced toward the sleeping man. "When your husband wakes up, tell him what he missed." He went through the door and closed it silently behind him.

Martha Ann put her face in her hands and cried.

Nine

"Oh, Lucky. My poor darling. Did you have a hard trip?"

"Well, honey, it wasn't so hard, but it just wasn't fast enough. I couldn't wait to get back home to my babies."

Martha Ann and Lucky and Evelyn were standing in the middle of the Tupelo Airport making a scene, which was par for the course for the Riley girls, Martha Ann thought. Evelyn had tears running down her cheeks, her mascara was streaked, and she was shouting. She always shouted when she was happy.

As for Lucky, he looked like death eating crackers, but he was patting Evelyn's stomach and grinning like a kid who had just gotten his hand caught in the cookie jar.

"If I could interrupt this domestic bliss long enough to say something—" Martha Ann was cut off by Evelyn.

"My poor baby." Evelyn cupped Lucky's face. "You shouldn't go off like that. I *worry* about you."

"You worry about *him*." Martha Ann was shouting, too, but she didn't care. The trip had been rough, and the times she hadn't been praying, she had been crying. She had lost her clothes, her money, her sense, and her heart, to boot, and all they could do was pet each other. "If somebody will tell me where the damned car is, I'll give *him* something to worry about."

"Why Martha Ann." Evelyn gave her a reproachful look. "You're cursing."

"Damned right. And hollering too."

Evelyn linked arms with her sister. "Poor baby. I know it's been rough for you too—Lucky, take her other arm. Let's get her to the car so she can put her head back and rest. . . . Quick. I think she's going to hyperventilate. She's scared to death of flying, poor thing."

It wasn't flying that had her so upset. It was Rick McGill. But she didn't tell Evelyn that. Her sister had enough to worry about without adding a failed romance to her list of woes.

As soon as they were in the car, Martha Ann had her say.

"Lucky O'Grady, if you ever go off like that again, I'll personally strip you buck naked and tan your selfish hide."

"Why, Martha Ann. I'm shocked at you." Evelyn patted her husband's cheek. "Keep your eyes on the road, baby. I'm sure she didn't mean that."

"You bet your sweet patooties, I did." Martha Ann leaned over the front seat and tapped Lucky's shoulder for emphasis. "You're a smart man, maybe even a brilliant one. Don't you think it's time you started using that brain to think up ways to be a good husband to my sister and a good father to my nephew?"

"Niece," Evelyn said. "It's going to be a girl."

"A girl?" Lucky beamed at her. "Honey, why didn't you tell me sooner . . . me, the father of a sweet little girl with pink ribbons in her hair. . . . How did you know, honey?"

"A mother-to-be just knows these things."

"Good grief. I give up." Martha Ann leaned her head against the backseat of the car.

By the time they were nearly to her house in Fulton, she had revived herself. She leaned over the seat again.

"Listen, Lucky. I like you—always have. It hurts me to see you keep doing this. And I *hate* what your leaving does to my sister."

Lucky reached for his wife's hand and lifted it to his lips. "I don't like to keep doing it, but I can't seem to help myself." He squeezed Evelyn's hand and shot her an affectionate glance. "That's why I've decided to enroll in Gamblers Anonymous."

"Oh, Lucky . . ."

"I was going to suggest that myself." Martha Ann chuckled. "Actually, I was going to insist, with a fencing sword if necessary."

Evelyn's laughter was shrill with relief and joy. "She's just teasing, honey. Martha Ann's really a sweetheart."

Sweetheart. The word burned through Martha Ann and seared her soul. Where was Rick McGill now? Had he stayed behind in Las Vegas or had he caught the first plane out? She hadn't seen him again after he'd brought Lucky to her room. Had it only been since six o'clock this morning? It seemed like forever.

Three hours after Rick had left them the clerk at the front desk had called to say her tickets were ready, and now there she was, back in Mississippi with her sister's runaway husband and a broken heart. The first thing she was going to do when she got home was buy a new rosary. She had a lot to talk over with the saints.

"Did you hear what I said?"

Martha Ann realized Evelyn was talking to her. "What?"

"I said, we're going to name the baby Lucy Ann, after you."

"Evelyn!" Tears came to her eyes. "I don't know what to say."

"Well . . . I didn't mean to make you cry. Lucky, say something funny, honey, I've gone and made my sister cry."

Martha Ann sniffed loudly and waved her hand in airy dismissal. "It's not you, Evelyn. I'm just tired, that's all."

She was still tired a week later. She had no idea jet lag lasted so long. That's what she had called it all week. Jet lag. It was easier to deal with than "broken heart."

She threw her uneaten toast out to the birds and scraped her half-eaten eggs down the garbage disposal. Then she went into the bathroom and looked at herself in the mirror.

The Bride of Dracula. That's who she looked like. She would probably scare her summer school students half to death. She squinted and contorted her eyes. Eye exercises. She'd read in a magazine at the beauty shop that every woman over thirty-five needed to do them.

She opened her eyes and looked at herself. She didn't see a darned bit of improvement. That just went to show that she couldn't believe every fool thing she read. The only good thing that had come out of that silly exercise was that she had forgotten about Rick McGill for all of three minutes. Good. It was a start.

She picked up her briefcase and headed toward the campus of Itawamba Community College.

Rick McGill stood in his office staring at the letter. He had been staring at it for the last five minutes.

Rick,
I want to thank you for helping me find Lucky O'Grady. As soon as I receive your bill, I will send payment in full. By the way, just so you won't think my sister is a sleazy woman, I want you to know that Lucky is really my brother-in-law. I posed as my sister because I thought it would be best that way.

> *Kind regards,*
> *Martha Ann Riley*

Kind regards. The knot he'd been carrying in the pit of his stomach for the last week pulled itself a little tighter. After all they'd been through together, all she could write was kind regards.

He threw the letter onto his desk and began to pace. After Martha Ann had left Las Vegas, he'd stayed a week longer to take care of his burned-out plane. Dealing with the insurance adjuster had helped keep that conniving woman off his mind. But now he was home, and thoughts of her were back in full force.

He stalked over to the desk and jerked the letter up. She wanted to pay in full, did she? Well, why not oblige the little lady?

He tore across his office, hung the "Out to Lunch" sign on his door, got in his car, and roared off toward Fulton. It was a small town. One conniving history professor shouldn't be too hard to find.

It was three o'clock when he found her.

She was standing at the front of her classroom, writing on the board. Rick leaned against the door-jamb and watched her. She was wearing a flirty little dress with a peplum that bounced when she moved. Her hair was as black and shiny as he remembered, and it swung with every movement of her head.

The knot in his stomach loosened a little, and his mouth quirked up at the corners.

"Your first assignment will be to read this chapter. . . ." The chalk squeaked as she scrawled the page numbers on the board. When she moved from behind the desk, Rick saw that she was wearing spike heels and hose with seams down the back. She looked like something out of the forties, and he had never been able to resist anything about the forties.

The quivering at his mouth became a full-fledged smile.

"Are there any questions?" Martha Ann turned to face her class.

That neon billboard Rick had been looking for suddenly lit up like a Fourth-of-July fireworks display. He was head-over-heels-by-george-crazy in love with Martha Ann Riley. His longtime goal of staying free till he was fifty vanished. Had it been a goal or just an excuse? It didn't matter anymore. All that mattered was love—and doing something about it.

He stepped away from the door and drawled, "Do I get extra points if I kiss the teacher?"

The students twittered.

Martha Ann put her hand over her heart. It was

pounding so hard at the sight of him. If he came one step closer, she thought, she'd make a fool of herself on the very first day of summer school, right in front of her entire class. She stepped back and clutched the edge of her desk for support.

"You'll have to leave, Mr. McGill. This class is in session."

"So am I, sweetheart. And this time I won't take no for an answer." With slow, deliberate movements, he stalked her.

There was a hushed silence in the room, and then a student in the back of the class shouted, "Dr. Riley, will this be on our first test?"

Bedlam broke loose. The girls giggled, and the boys whooped and hollered and clapped their hands. A few of the braver ones shouted encouragement to Rick.

"We're on your side, Mr. McGill."

"Hey, did you see the teach blush? I think she likes you."

"I think I'm going to *love* History 101."

Martha Ann stuck out her chin and tried to take control. "This class is dismissed." There was a general charge for the door. "And don't forget to read your assignment."

"What's my assignment, teach?" Rick McGill propped one lean hip on her desk and smiled at her.

"To go back where you came from."

"Sweetheart, I'm afraid it's too late for that."

"Why?" Her knees were weak, her heart was fluttering, and she was whispering.

"Because, my pet . . ." He straightened up and walked around the desk. Putting one hand on her chin, he tipped her face up to his. ". . . I'm in love."

Martha Ann wanted to scream. She wanted to melt all over him like an ice-cream cone left too long in the hot sun, and she wanted to bash him with her history book.

"Give the lady my congratulations."

His big boom of laughter echoed around the now-empty classroom.

"You never give up, do you, sweetheart?"

"You've tried everything else to get me into your bed. I'm an intelligent woman. Why did you expect to come marching in here and have me fall hook, line and sinker for that story?"

"Because it's true."

She was speechless. She wanted to believe him and yet she knew what he was. How could she give herself to an avowed playboy?

"Hold on to that thought, my pet." He released her, walked to the door, and pushed it shut. The click of the lock sounded loud in the quiet room. Next he walked over to the side of the room and pulled all the window shades down.

She was paralyzed. He was temptation so great she was panting. A sane, sensible side of her mind told her to resist, and a crazy, impulsive side told her to run, not walk, into his arms.

He saved her the trouble.

As soon as the last shade was down, he strode behind the desk and pulled her roughly against his chest. "Let's see if you've forgotten how to kiss."

When his lips touched hers, such sweet tenderness swept through her that she thought she would die. Right there in her classroom among the history books and the chalk dust.

"Hmmm." He lifted his head and smiled at her. "You remembered. I'm so glad." His mouth came down on hers again.

She was melting, she was turning to butter, she was going to fall to the middle of her hardwood floor. Had there ever been a man as persuasive as Rick McGill? She was certain there hadn't.

"Ahhh . . ." Her head tipped back. "Don't do this to me."

His lips skimmed her neck. "We do it to each other. . . . Sweet, you taste so sweet." One hand spread across her hips and dragged her closer.

He took her breath away. She curled her hands into his hair and pressed his head down.

"Please, Rick . . . please."

"Sweetheart . . ." With one hand he unbuttoned the front of her dress. "Oh, baby . . . my sweet pet . . ." His tongue wet her nipple through the white lace bra. She groaned.

He took the hardened nipple deep in his mouth, lace and all. Her hips began a small rhythm against his. She couldn't help herself. She knew that classes were over for the day, but fifteen million students could have been banging at her door, the Dean to boot, and she would still have done what she was doing.

"I can . . . never . . . love . . . a conniving rake . . . ahhhh, please. Do that again."

He nudged the lace aside and teased her erect nipple with his teeth and tongue. Shivers went down her spine. Groaning, he lifted his head and took her mouth. All the savage hunger of a man who wouldn't be denied was there.

She surrendered. With lips and tongue she encouraged him, moaning and murmuring her pleasure.

He caught her skirt with his hand and inched it upward. When his fingers made contact with naked flesh, Rick chuckled deep in his throat.

"A garter belt, my pet? You delight me." He spread his palm over her thigh, rubbing it in erotic circles.

"That feels . . . soooo good . . . ahhhh, Rick. . . ."

"Does this?" His fingers inched her lace panties *aside*. "*. . . and this? . . . Don't answer that, my pet.* I can tell." His expert fingers continued their ministrations.

The room seemed to whirl around her. Time was suspended. Nothing existed except the exquisite pleasure of Rick McGill.

Finally it wasn't enough—for either of them.

He unhooked her garters and slid her stockings down her legs. They drifted to the floor, then he slipped off her lace panties.

Her hands fumbled with his belt buckle. "One time," she whispered. "Just this once . . . and then . . ."

His pants hit the floor. "And then forever, sweetheart." He lifted her up and braced her hips against the desk. His first thrust was swift and sure. When he was fully buried in her moist warm flesh, he let out a sigh. "Ahhh, sweetheart. I'm home."

She clutched his back. "Don't . . . talk. . . ."

The sweet jazzy rhythm of love began. Her fingernails dug into his back.

"Rick!"

"Easy, sweetheart. We have the rest of our lives."

Her heart banged against her rib cage and sweat trickled between her breasts and she was in heaven. She clung to him, half-crazy with ecstasy. Her entire existence seemed centered in that moment. All her yesterdays and all her tomorrows came together in one golden hour.

And when it was over, he kissed her until her pulse slowed back to normal. Then he slipped into his pants, picked up her panties and her hose, and dressed her with tender care.

Still kneeling in front of her, he took her hand. "Will you marry me, Martha Ann Riley?"

She put her hands to her flushed cheeks and tried to think straight. But she couldn't. All she could do was stall for time.

"I can't marry you. I don't know you."

"I'm a lonely old bachelor living in a big old house in Tupelo, but I'm perfectly willing to live anywhere in the world as long as you're there."

His disarming candor enchanted her. She decided to play his game. "What about your work?"

"I can take it or leave it. I'm what folks call filthy rich."

"From Colombian emeralds?"

"Yes."

"And bordellos?"

He tipped back his head and roared with laughter. "Where did you hear that?"

"Somewhere in Tupelo."

"You're too smart to believe everything you hear."

"Then it's not true?"

"I've been wicked in my time, but not that wicked. If you promise not to tell anyone . . ." He leaned closer and kissed her knees. "My bordellos are nothing more than ordinary stocks and bonds. Tame stuff."

"I can't think when you kiss my knees."

"Good." He braced her foot on his knee, pushed up her dress, and planted long, lingering kisses on her inner thigh.

"Please, Rick."

"Sweetheart, I believe we're going to have to undress you again." His voice was hoarse and thick as he unsnapped her garter belt. Her hose and panties whispered down her legs.

He stripped off his pants, sat in her swivel chair, and pulled her down on top of him.

She sighed.

He captured her mouth, and her passion spiraled quickly. The chair rocked back and forth and from time to time threatened to tumble over. They laughed and murmured sweet love words into each others' ears.

Summer dusk fell over the campus, and still Rick and Martha Ann loved. The chair had gotten too confining, and they moved to the floor. It was hard and dusty, but neither of them noticed.

At last Rick propped himself on one elbow and gazed down at her.

"The next time we're going to try this on a soft bed . . ." He looked ruefully at her half-open blouse and his unbuttoned shirt. ". . . and without any clothes."

She opened her mouth to speak, and he covered it with his own. "If you say 'There won't be a next time,' I'm going to spank your bare bottom."

His words were mumbled against her lips, but she knew exactly what he was saying.

"Rick . . ."

"What, my pet?"

"You're going to have to let me up. I have a seven o'clock faculty meeting."

"I can't."

"Why?"

"You haven't said yes."

"I can't say yes—but I can't say no either."

"That will do."

He stood up and held out his hand. She pulled herself up and began to straighten her clothes.

"I must look a sight."

"You look like a woman who has been thoroughly loved."

"That's what I was afraid of." She went to her desk and got her lipstick out of her purse. "Good grief. Look at the time." It was six forty-five. "Rick McGill, you're going to ruin my reputation."

"All the more reason for agreeing to let me make an honest woman of you."

She jerked her comb out of her purse and ran it hastily through her hair. "I told you, I'm not going to agree to such a thing. . . . Where are my stockings?"

Grinning, he picked them up off the floor and handed them to her. She quickly put them on and snapped her garters.

"Wow 'em, sweetheart," he called as she hurried out the door. It banged shut behind her, and he went whistling toward her desk. A tiny wisp of white caught his eye. "Well, well. What have we here?" He reached down to her desk and snagged the object between his thumb and forefinger. It was Martha Ann's white lace panties.

Still whistling, he stuffed them into his pants pocket.

"Dr. Riley?"

She jumped. Good grief, Dr. Bluebakker was scowling at her as if she had circulated copies of his English 205 exam. Could he possibly guess that she was sitting at the faculty meeting without any panties? She bit her bottom lip and tried to get a grip on herself.

"Yes, Dr. Bluebakker?"

"I've asked you *three* times already what you thought about the Sixth Annual Lecture Series? Do you agree that we should invite that local romance novelist to address our student body?"

Martha Ann perked up. "You mean Peggy Webb? I think she would be an excellent choice. You know, there's been a lot of interest and a lot of good writing in that genre." She was feeling proud of herself for holding it all together. She leaned back in her chair and relaxed. "By the way, what's the date for our sex series?"

"Dr. RILEY!" Dr. Raymond Bluebakker looked shocked, but the rest of the faculty burst into laughter.

"Loosen up, Raymond," Dr. Simeon Jonas said. "We've been in this damned meeting too long anyhow. It's time to go home."

The meeting broke up after that, and Martha Ann was the first one out the door. She'd kill Rick McGill when she saw him again.

She couldn't, of course. When he turned up the next morning at her house, all she could do was smile.

He propped one foot on her doorstep and gave her the wickedest grin this side of the Mississippi. "I believe I have something you want."

She still hadn't made up her mind about him, so she decided to play it cool. "You don't have a thing I can't live without."

"I would keep 'em, sweetheart, but they're not my size." Grinning, he pulled her panties out of his pocket.

"If that's not just like you to hold my panties hostage while I'm sitting barebottomed in the faculty meeting."

"Yes. It's just like me." He stuffed the panties back into his pocket. "We'll have to do it more often."

"We most certainly will not."

He came up the steps two at a time and pulled her into his arms. "Dr. Riley, my pet, do you know how cute you are when you're playacting?"

"I'm not playacting. I'm darned good and mad."

"There's but one cure for that." He bent her over backward and kissed her.

Old Mrs. Glenell Swan next door was just coming onto her front porch to get her morning paper. When she saw what was going on, she stopped to take it all in. The man was as handsome as any she'd seen on the TV. And there was her neighbor, that cute Martha Ann Riley, dressed in nothing but her pink cotton batiste nightgown and robe, getting kissed like one of those TV soap opera heroines. She looked like she was enjoying it too.

Mrs. Swan stood there for a while, and when it looked as if they were going to go on all day, she pulled up her lawn chair and sat down so her arthritis wouldn't pain her. She didn't want to miss a thing.

She scooted her chair toward the edge of her porch and leaned toward her neighbor's house. The morning traffic hadn't started over on the highway, and the air was still and quiet. If she listened real hard, maybe she could hear what was being said.

Rick took one last long, heady taste of Martha Ann, and then he released her. And not a second too soon, he decided. A little while longer and he would have taken her on her own front porch.

"That's not a cure. That's an assault." Martha Ann stepped back and tried to regain control of the situation.

"In Tupelo we call it good morning."

"In Fulton we call it scandalous."

"I think it's nice." The quavery old voice wafting across the way made them both jump. Mrs. Swan rose from her chair, grinning and waving. "Howdy do, Martha Ann? I see you got yourself a nice new beau."

"This is Rick McGill, Mrs. Swan. But he's not a beau; he's just a friend."

"Yes, I am, Mrs. Swan. And I'm planning to be her husband." Rick was in a jovial mood. "You're invited to the wedding."

"When?" the old lady asked.

"As soon as I can persuade her to marry me."

Mrs. Swan giggled. "Young man, it seems to me you've got a powerful method of persuasion. Good luck to ya." She bent down and got her morning paper, then tottered back inside.

Rick took Martha Ann's elbow and led her into her house, talking all the while. "The neighbors approve, sweetheart. What more could you want?"

"A few answers for starters." He nuzzled her ear. "From the other side of the room. I can't think straight when you do that."

"Anything for my sassy forties lady." He straddled a wooden chair on the far side of a sunny room that was a combination study and den with a small kitchen nook.

Martha Ann went to her refrigerator and took out a pitcher of orange juice. She poured two glasses and carried one over to him. "And make it short. I have a nine o'clock class."

"What do you want to know?"

She took a fortifying gulp of juice. "All that time we were in the Valley of Fire . . ."

"Memorable, wasn't it?"

". . . and all those times in Velma's bed . . ."

"I love it when you blush."

"Just hush up a minute and let me think." She set her glass on the cabinet and turned her back to him. "I can't think when you look at me like that."

"Like what?"

"You know . . . with those bedroom eyes."

He chuckled.

"It should be against the law for a blond-haired man to have such dark eyes." She raked her hand through her hair. "I swear, you're going to drive me to cuss." Suddenly she remembered her outburst in the airport. "Already have, as a matter of fact."

"Sweetheart, I don't mean to make this hard." He sounded contrite. The chair scrapped as he stood up.

She whirled around. "Stay right where you are." Her hand shook as she picked up her glass. "I declare, Rick McGill, I don't know whether you are a scoundrel or a saint."

"A little bit of both, I'm afraid."

His smile was so endearing, she almost gave up on trying to create order out of chaos. Watching him, she drained her glass and set it on the counter.

"Just when did you first know that I wasn't married?"

"Ahhh. You want to know if I deliberately set out to seduce a married woman?"

"Yes."

His face became serious. "I've known from the beginning, Martha Ann."

She wavered between being relieved and being enraged. The rage won. Batting the air with her fists for emphasis, she stalked around the room. "Isn't that just like a man? Toying with a woman's feelings for the heck of it. I should have known. All of you are just alike."

"So, I'm being lumped with the less-than-saintly Marcus Grimes." Rick's voice was tight.

Martha Ann stopped her pacing and whirled in on him. "How did you know about him?"

"Any private investigator worth his salt would find out all about the woman he planned to seduce."

Martha Ann failed to notice the hard edge in his voice and the deadly calm in his eyes.

"So, you admit it. It was just a seduction all along."

"It started out that way." He stepped around the serving bar and caught her shoulders. "But it turned into something else."

"Love?"

"Yes, love."

"How very convenient for you."

"Not convenient." His grip tightened. "Not convenient at all. And certainly not easy." He caught her chin with one hand and forced her to look into his eyes. "Dammit, Martha Ann—See, you've got me cussing too." His fingers caressed her jaw. "Sweetheart, I know you're mad, and you have every right to be. But remember, I wasn't the only one carrying on a little charade."

"I had my reasons."

"I'd like to hear them." The harshness was gone from his face, his voice. "Talk to me, sweetheart."

She was shaky inside, both from her mixed-up feelings and from the nearness of Rick. Oh heavens, she thought. She *did* love him so.

"The Riley girls don't have any sense about men. Never did."

"Marcus and Lucky. I see your point."

"And then there was that last goober I dated. He was nothing but a common, two-bit swindler."

"I don't swindle and I don't steal, and the only excuse I have for not telling you that I knew the truth was that I decided to play your game and have some fun."

Her lips quivered, then twitched, then turned up in a smile that was pure nostalgia. "We did have fun, didn't we?"

"Yes." He gazed into her eyes. "You're a delightful

woman, Martha Ann Riley. A funny, sassy, bright, passionate woman. And I want to spend the rest of my life with you."

"Rick." Her hand touched his cheek. "It's not that I don't love you—I do—I've known it for a long, long time, perhaps since that first day I walked into your office."

"You too?"

"Yes. I've never believed in love at first sight before."

"Neither have I. It just goes to show you that love is stronger than skepticism."

"Ahhh, Rick." She rested her head against his shoulder. He tangled his hands in her hair.

"Take your time, sweetheart. My love's not going to go away."

From a distance they could hear the muffled growl and roar of the early morning traffic, like beasts being dragged reluctantly through a concrete jungle.

Martha Ann lifted her head. "I have to go to class."

He kissed her forehead. "I'll miss you, sweetheart."

Ten

It was that tender kiss on her forehead that she was still thinking about when she dismissed her last class for the day. Thank goodness it was over. Her concentration had been fractured, to say the least.

She sank into her swivel chair and began to sort papers. Some she would take home in her briefcase, others she would file. How was a woman to know when to trust a man and when not to? Pressing her fingers over her eyes, she leaned back in her chair. Love was all well and good, but she was too old and too wise not to know that there were other considerations in a marriage. Trust. Dependability. Maturity. Oh, help. All that sounded like the qualifications for a good stockbroker.

She just wasn't going to think about it anymore. She rose from her chair, smoothed down her skirt, and picked up her briefcase. Thank heaven, Rick hadn't interrupted her school day. Apparently he meant what he said about letting her take her time.

She was going straight home and curl up with a good book and spend two or three hours not thinking at all. Sometimes that was the best way to solve a problem.

She was well into that good book, when she heard the commotion at her front door. It wasn't a knocking or even a call 'hello.' It was pure, unadulterated racket.

"What in the world?" She put a bookmark on page sixty-five, closed the book, and walked toward her front door. She had left the wooden door open so she could catch the late afternoon breeze through the screen. What she saw through the screen made her laugh until her sides hurt.

Rick McGill was on her front porch dressed in fringed leather britches, beaded moccasins, and a huge feathered headdress. He held a boom box in one hand and a very large, very full mesh bag in the other. On the radio the Andrew Sisters were singing 'Boogie Woogie Bugle Boy" two decibels too loud, and Rick was doing a combination Texas two-step and Indian rain dance.

When he saw her, he grinned.

"What are you doing?" She had to yell to make herself heard over all the racket.

"It's a little Indian love dance." He executed a few steps. He did a few more. "Do you like it?"

Her laughter turned into a smile of endearment. Only Rick McGill would dance so badly and then expect her to like it.

"It's wonderful. Where did you learn it?"

"I made it up all by myself." He stomped clumsily around the porch again, whistling and humming and sometimes grinning.

"Don't you think the music is wrong for that kind of dance?"

"No. Forties music always suits the occasion. I think we should play it at our wedding."

He was absolutely incorrigible. She went through the screen door and stood in front of him, arms akimbo. "I guess you're going to keep up this racket until I invite you in."

"That's right."

"And all my neighbors will hate me."

"They might even circulate petitions to get you to move in with me."

"In that case . . ." She held the screen door wide. "Do come in."

He turned the music down to a soft croon and went into her front room. The big sack in his hand bumped against the door frame.

Martha Ann moved her book out of the way and sat back down in her comfortable chair. "What's in the bag?"

"A love potion."

"You're kidding."

"I made it myself too." He set the boom box on the kitchen counter and held up the huge bag. "If that little thing Clyde made could do what it did, just think what this sucker can do."

"It boggles the mind." She was enchanted. That's all there was to it, she thought. Such considerations as reliability and stability and trustworthiness flew right out the door in the face of this crazy, wonderful man with his love potion.

"Of course, in order to work, this potion has to be put in exactly the right place."

"Naturally."

"You do have a bed, don't you?"

Her pulse began to race. Without a word, she got up and locked her front door. She leaned against the doorjamb for support. "Do you think it will fit?"

His eyes went dark. "I'm certain it will fit."

She blushed. He noticed. A slow, lazy smile spread across his face.

"Why don't we give it a try?" He held out his left hand, and she took it.

Together they went into her bedroom. It was small and cozy, decorated with lots of wicker and brass and handmade pillows and art noveau prints. The room was like her, he thought. Both old-fashioned and sweet, and wildly modern and bold.

She stood in the middle of the room and folded her hands neatly across her breasts. "This morning you told me to take my time."

"This morning was a million years ago." He put the bag on the floor and went to her. Reaching out, he touched her cheek with one hand. "I couldn't stay away."

"I can't make up my mind."

"I'll help you." Gazing deep into her eyes, he began to unbutton her blouse. He took his time, savoring every precious moment. When he had slid it from her shoulders, he stood back admiring her. "You have the most beautiful shoulders in the world." He leaned down and kissed them, first one and then the other. "Worthy of a poem or two."

To her amazement he began to quote the Song of Songs. She held her breath, afraid that one single move, one single sound would stop the magic. His voice rose in deep splendor as he quoted:

Rise up, my darling; my fairest, come away.
For now the winter is past,
the rains are over and gone;
the flowers appear in the countryside;
the time is coming when the birds will sing,
and the turtledoves' cooing will be heard in our
    land,

*when the green figs will ripen on the fig trees
and the vines give forth their fragrance.
Rise up, my darling;
my fairest, come away.*

She trembled, still hesitant to speak and break
the spell. Without a word he unhooked her skirt and
slid it over her hips. Then, with tender care, he
knelt before her, unfastened her garter belt, and
began to roll down her stockings. He lifted his eyes
to hers as he hooked his thumbs in the waistband
of her panties and slid them down her legs.

"I'm still not making any promises," she whispered.

"I am." He eased her legs apart and kissed her
inner thigh. "For the first time in my life I'm willing
to make promises." He put his hands on her but-
tocks and urged her closer.

"Ahhh, Rick." Her head fell back. White hot sensations shot through her. Blindly, she reached down
and caught his hair, tugging him close, urging him
on.

The room tipped upside down. All the colors of the
rainbow swirled before her eyes. A storm center built
in her and spread. She cried out.

Rick lifted her and carried her to the bed. She lay
with her hair fanned across the pillows and her
back pressed flat against the log cabin quilt, gazing
up at him. He took his time undressing, making a
sensuous show of it.

With the late afternoon shadows making dark
patches on his chest and shading his face in mystery, he was glorious. She lifted her arms, and he
came to her.

His entry was slow and sweet. There was no need
to hurry. The day was almost over, they had nowhere to go, and the bed was soft and inviting. So

was she, he thought. So was she. *Warm* and soft and inviting. The music of a thousand golden oldies played through his soul. And he danced to it.

It was a love dance that lasted until they were both sated and sweaty. Afterward they lay tangled in each other's arms.

She leaned on one elbow and gazed tenderly down at him. "You never did show me what was in that bag."

His smile was slow and lazy and satisfied. "It worked, didn't it?"

She grinned. "So . . . that's what's been seducing me all evening? A big old love potion."

"Big, sweetheart, but not so old." He ran his fingers through her hair. "I figure I have at least a hundred years of loving left in me."

"Is that a fact? That will be one for the history books."

He pulled her face down to his. "Let's make a little more history, teach."

Their mouths were love-slick and puffy. What started as a series of sweet, teasing kisses soon escalated.

Rick growled deep in his throat and pulled her on top of him. When he was fully sheathed once more, he began a wild, plunging rhythm. No sweet, slow music this time. They made the frenzied love of two people who thought they might never get enough of each other.

It was quick and hard and fast and explosive.

Later, Rick got off the bed and unfastened his "love potion." First he pulled a flat white florist's box out of the mesh bag and handed it to her.

She opened the lid and took out a dozen red roses. She buried her face in the fragrant petals.

"I haven't had roses since I was in college."

She was genuinely touched. It would be just like that wonderful man to have known. After all, he seemed to know everything else about her. And what he didn't know he was rapidly finding out.

Smiling, she got a vase and put the roses in water. He came up behind her and circled her waist.

"Sweetheart, I intend to give you roses every day for the rest of your life." He reached into the bag and pulled out a bottle. "And champagne." He reached in again. "And bread . . . and grapes."

She was laughing again. Rick always made her laugh. "Grapes?"

"Absolutely. Don't you know this is the fruit of love?"

"Do we *need* fruit?"

"Are you questioning a gift horse?" He plucked a grape and put it between his teeth. Moving in close, he offered it to her. She bit into it, and the juice dribbled down her chin. Rick licked it off.

"Hmmmm," she said. "Some fruit."

"Hmmmm. Some body." He squeezed a handful of grapes over her breasts and stood back to watch the tangy juice trickle over her nipples. "How can I resist?" He spent a long, leisurely time enjoying the juice.

"My turn." She took a handful of grapes and squeezed them on his chest. Her tongue flicked at the juice. "Hmmm, delicious."

He uncorked the champagne and unwrapped the bread. They climbed onto the bed and fed each other bits of bread and sips of champagne straight from the bottle.

A long while later she said, "I could get glasses."

"Where are they?"

"In the kitchen."

"Sweetheart, that's much too faraway. I can't let you leave on that long journey."

She fell back on the bed, laughing. He took advantage of her position to reach for a bunch of grapes and drizzle the juice on her thighs. His eyes gleamed as he bent over her to lick away the juice.

"My dear, you *do* know how to serve a man his fruit."

"Rick . . . ohhhh, my."

"If a man . . . is going . . . to get . . . side-tracked . . ." He rolled onto his back, taking her with him. ". . . this is the way . . . to do it."

While they were sidetracked, the sun disappeared from the sky. The room turned dark and cozy, and it was filled with the pungent smell of grapes and champagne and roses and love.

She lay atop him, limp and panting. When the phone rang, it took her a few seconds to realize where the noise was coming from. She thought it might be her overheated blood boiling and her heart hammering.

"Are you expecting a call, sweetheart?"

"No."

"Let it go then." He pressed his lips to the side of her throat.

The phone continued its insistent jangling.

"It might be important." Martha Ann rolled off him and picked up the receiver.

"Hello," she said.

"Martha Ann? Is that you? You sound funny."

It was Evelyn. Martha Ann cleared her throat and tried for a more businesslike tone.

"Of course, it's me."

"What are you doing?"

"What am I doing?" She echoed aloud.

Rick leaned over and kissed her abdomen. "Making Michael."

"Hush." She swatted him away.

"What's that, Martha Ann?"

"Nothing. I was just clearing my throat." She cleared her throat loudly. Rick chuckled.

"Now don't get excited or anything. . . ."

"I'm *not* excited." But she was beginning to get irritated. Why didn't Evelyn get to the point?

"Oh, yes you are, my sweet," Rick murmured against her breast. "And exciting too."

"Stop that." Martha Ann playfully punched his chest.

"What?"

"Not you, Evelyn."

"Martha Ann, what in the world's going on?"

Martha Ann took a deep, exasperated breath. Goodness gracious. Sometimes the Riley girls were as dense as they could be. "You're the one who called, Evelyn. You tell me."

"Don't get excited . . ."

If Evelyn said that one more time, she was going to scream.

". . . but I'm in the hospital."

Martha Ann sat bolt upright. "In the hospital?"

"Here in Pontotoc. It seems Lucy Ann has decided to come early."

Martha Ann already had her feet over the side of the bed and was reaching for her underwear. "Listen, don't you dare have that baby till I get there. Do you hear?"

"Well, I'll try." Evelyn giggled, then groaned. "But you might hurry. It seems that Lucy Ann has a mind of her own."

"I'll be right there." She jerked on her blouse and buttoned it up crooked.

"What's wrong?" Rick was already out of bed pulling on his pants.

"We're having a baby!"

"Not yet, sweetheart, but we will. I can guarantee that."

Rick refastened Martha Ann's buttons and handed her the hairbrush, which she swore had disappeared to China, and finally got her out to his car in one piece.

"I'll drive," he said. "I don't think nervous aunts should be allowed on the road."

By the time they arrived at the hospital, Lucy Ann O'Grady had already made her debut.

Evelyn was propped up in bed, holding the tiny red-faced baby girl, and Lucky was standing by the bedside beaming.

Martha Ann, dressed in hospital gown and mask, started cooing the minute she saw her niece. "Just look at her. She has my chin." She motioned to Rick, who was standing just inside the door. "Don't you think she has my chin?"

He crossed the room, held out his finger, and the tiny hand closed around it. He was immediately smitten. "That's the first thing I noticed. She definitely has your beautiful, stubborn chin."

"And look at her eyes, Rick. Don't you think they look like mine?"

He gazed from Martha Ann to the baby and back. "I do believe she does. Lucky little girl."

"Look at the size of those little feet. I believe she's going to be a tall girl—just like me."

Evelyn smiled and winked at Lucky. "The next thing you know, she's going to be claiming all the credit."

He chuckled. "Sorry about that, Martha Ann. This one's ours. You're going to have to have your own baby."

"And when you do, I'm going to be there with bells on saying she looks just like me," Evelyn chimed in. Her sister leaned closer and cooed to the baby. "Does anybody in this room smell grapes?"

Martha Ann and Rick both jumped and looked at each other.

"Seems I do," Lucky said. "Been smelling them from the minute you two walked in the door."

"Well, I'm trying out a new bubble bath."

"It must be a new room spray."

Rick and Martha Ann spoke up at the same time. Then they grinned at each other.

"You go ahead," Martha Ann said. "Your story sounds better than mine."

He cleared his throat loudly. "There's just no accounting for the room sprays they use in hospitals these days to kill the antiseptic smell."

Everybody laughed. Then Lucky handed Rick a cigar, and they went downstairs to the lounge so they could smoke and Lucky could brag.

As soon as the men had gone, Evelyn gave her sister a thorough once-over. "Congratulations, Martha Ann."

"What are you talking about, Evelyn? You're the one who has just had the baby."

"I'm talking about those wedding bells I hear. And don't try to tell me he hasn't asked."

"He has."

"And?"

"And . . . I told him I needed time."

"Time won't change a thing."

The sisters looked at each other in perfect understanding.

Suddenly Martha Ann smiled. "You are right. You are so right!" She whirled around and started for the door, pulling off her hospital gown and mask as she went.

"Tell him I think a little Scottish blood is just what you need to tame that Irish in you," Evelyn called after her.

Martha Ann laughed and waved and kept on going. She found Rick in the lounge, stretched out on a love seat, pretending to enjoy his cigar. Lucky was sitting in a nearby chair talking about Lucy Ann's first piano recital.

She paused just inside the door, propped one hand on her hip, and winked at Rick.

His eyes lit up, and he pulled the big cigar out of his mouth. "By george, I always did love a woman who could pose."

"Get used to it, sweetheart," she said, imitating his Humphrey Bogart drawl. "I'm going to be posing for you for the rest of my life."

"Does that mean what I think it means?"

"Evelyn says to tell you welcome to the family, you big Scottish scoundrel."

Watching her, Rick took a big draw on his cigar and blew out a ring of smoke. "Not afraid of swindlers and thieves and blackmailers and such, are you?"

"With you, I don't think I ever was." She walked slowly across the room, undulating her hips in a manner he found exceedingly sexy. When she was only a few feet from him, she stopped. "This time around, my marriage will be built on complete trust—till death do us part."

Rick took another long, satisfying puff of his cigar. Suddenly he was enjoying it very much. It seemed just right for celebrating a marriage. He blew three more smoke rings in the air.

"If you'll come a little closer, sweetheart, we'll seal the bargain."

She advanced on him, a vampish pout on her lips and a gleam in her eye. When she reached the love seat, she stood in front of him and held out her hand.

"With a handshake, of course," she said, deadpan.

"Naturally." He took her hand and gave it a solemn shake. Then he gave a tug that sent her tumbling onto his lap.

"Rick, this is a hospital!"

"The perfect place to be." He gave her a quick but thorough kiss. "After I'm finished with you, we might both be in need of medical attention." He took her lips again.

Both of them had forgotten Lucky, but that didn't matter, for he had forgotten them also. He was talking to the walls now, describing Lucy Ann's first prom dress.

Six weeks later a large crowd was gathered inside the Episcopalian Church in Tupelo. Up front, Jacob Donovan, Rick's best friend, and Andrew McGill, his youngest brother, were lighting the candles. Evelyn was seated at the organ, playing a soft tune.

In the third pew from the front, Velma and Clyde Running Bear, who had flown in compliments of the groom, were whispering.

"That sounds like 'Boogie Woogie Bugle Boy' to me, Clyde."

"I guess they can play anything they want to. It's their wedding." He craned his neck to see if he could be the first one to catch a glimpse of the bride. "I think I see her, Velma."

"Shhh. Everybody's going to hear you."

Clyde turned back around and tried to look solemn. His solemnity lasted until Martha Ann Riley started down the aisle. Then he tugged on Velma's arm.

"I knew that love potion would work."

"Shhh, honey. Here comes the bride." They swiveled their heads around to watch Martha Ann. When the bride was at the front of the church, Velma leaned close to Clyde and whispered, "Are you *sure* you put it in the right place?"

"Trust me, Velma. I took care of everything."

Rick and Martha Ann left the church directly after the wedding and boarded his private plane. Then they headed for the Valley of Fire.

They landed there just at sunset. While Rick gathered firewood, Martha Ann unrolled their sleeping bags on the exact bluff top that had sheltered them during their quest for Lucky.

Rick came up behind her and circled his arms around her waist.

"Is that any way to begin a honeymoon, Mrs. McGill? Separate sleeping bags?"

She turned around and draped her arms around his neck. "I think the honeymoon started the last time we were here. Remember?"

"I remember everything about that night, including how hard these rocks felt."

She grinned. "Then why do you suppose we're here instead of in some nice hotel with a nice comfortable bed and nice clean sheets?"

"I hate *nice*." He kissed her.

"So do I."

"Do you think we should try naughty?"

"We always have." He bent over and picked up her sleeping bag. "Let me put this superfluous bedding away."

He gave the bag a brisk shake and out rolled a small, smelly mesh bag.

"It looks like our friend Clyde Running Bear has been at it again." He picked up the love potion, grinning.

"It worked the first time, didn't it?"

"It did, but, sweetheart, I don't relish the idea of keeping a bag of dead cow's ears in our bedroom for the rest of our lives."

"The rest of our lives. That has a nice ring."

"It certainly does. Come here, Mrs. McGill."

Martha Ann walked into her husband's arms, and the small mesh bag went sailing over the edge of the bluff.

Epilogue

"How could you do this to me, Martha Ann?"

"I had a little help."

Evelyn pushed past her brother-in-law to get a better look at the babies. Three of them. And all of them boys.

Martha Ann held on to the soft bundles and smiled. "Evelyn, meet Michael and his brothers. Say hello to your auntie, boys." Michael began to squall.

"Here. He wants his daddy." Rick McGill reached down and scooped one of the tiny infants into his arms. "Don't you cry, big fellow. Daddy's going to sing you a song." He began crooning 'Boogie Woogie Bugle Boy" off-key.

"Isn't he wonderful?" Martha Ann said to her sister.

"Well, if you ask me, he would have been more wonderful if he had fathered at least one girl." She leaned closer and inspected her sister's babies. "However, little Mark does have a mouth that looks suspiciously like mine." She picked up the baby and posed with him. "What do you think?"

"The spitting image of you," Martha Ann said.

"And I do believe his hair is going to be blond like mine."

"Without a doubt." Martha Ann winked at her husband. He winked back.

"Of course, I think little Matthew is going to have that stubborn Riley cowlick." Evelyn leaned down and swapped babies. "Just like mine." She cooed a little baby talk to Matthew, and then handed him to his proud daddy. "I'd say you did well for the first time around. Next time, though, I'm expecting you to present me with three nieces."

"I promise," he said.

Evelyn kissed each of her nephews on the top of his head, then left the new parents alone.

Rick came to the bed and sat down on the edge.

"Three girls?" Martha Ann smiled at him.

"Three girls." He bent and kissed his wife soundly on the lips. "And I never make promises I don't plan to keep, sweetheart."

THE EDITOR'S CORNER

We suspect that Cupid comes to visit our Bantam offices every year when we're preparing the Valentine's Day books. It seems we're always specially inspired by the one exclusively romantic holiday in the year. And our covers next month reflect just how inspired we were ... by our authors who also must have had a visit from the chubby cherub. They shimmer with cherry-red metallic ink and are presents in and of themselves—as are the stories within. They range from naughty to very nice!

First, we bring you Suzanne Forster's marvelous **WILD CHILD**, LOVESWEPT #384. Cat D'Angelo had been the town's bad girl and Blake Wheeler its golden boy when the young assistant D.A. had sent her to the reformatory for suspected car theft. Now, ten years later, she has returned to work as a counselor to troubled kids—and to even the score with the man who had hurt her so deeply! Time had only strengthened the powerful forces that drew them together ... and Blake felt inescapable hunger for the beautiful, complicated hellcat who could drive a man to ruin—or to ecstasy. Could the love and hate Cat had held so long in her heart be fused by the fire of mutual need and finally healed by passion? We think you'll find **WILD CHILD** delicious—yet calorie free—as chocolates packaged in a red satin box!

Treat yourself to a big bouquet with Gail Douglas's *The Dreamweavers:* **BEWITCHING LADY**, LOVESWEPT #385. When the Brawny Josh Campbell who looked as if he could wield a sword as powerfully as any clansman stopped on a deserted road to give her a ride, Heather Sinclair played a mischievous Scottish lass to the hilt, beguiling the moody but fascinating man whose gaze hid inner demons ... and hinted at a dangerous passion she'd never known. Josh felt his depression lift after months of despair, but he was too cynical to succumb to this delectable minx's appeal ... or was he? A true delight!

Sweet, fresh-baked goodies galore are yours in Joan

(continued)

Elliott Pickart's **MIXED SIGNALS,** LOVESWEPT #386. Katha Logan threw herself into Vince Santini's arms, determined to rescue the rugged ex-cop from the throng of reporters outside city hall. Vince enjoyed being kidnapped by this lovely and enchanting nut who drove like a madwoman and intrigued him with her story of a crime he just *had* to investigate . . . with her as his partner! Vince believed that a man who risked his life for a living had no business falling in love. Katha knew she could cherish Vince forever if he'd let her, but playing lovers' games wasn't enough anymore. Could they learn to fly with the angels and together let their passions soar?

We give a warm, warm greeting—covered with hearts, with flowers—to a new LOVESWEPT author, but one who's not new to any of us who treasure romances. Welcome Lori Copeland, who brings us LOVESWEPT #387, **DARLING DECEIVER,** next month. Bestselling mystery writer Shae Malone returned to the sleepy town where he'd spent much of his childhood to finish his new novel, but instead of peace and quiet, he found his home invaded by a menagerie of zoo animals temporarily living next door . . . with gorgeously grown-up Harriet Whitlock! As a teenager she'd chased him relentlessly, embarrassed him with poems declaring everlasting love, but now she was an exquisite woman whose long-legged body made him burn with white-hot fire. Harri still wanted Shae with shameless abandon, but did she dare risk giving her heart again?

Your temperature may rise when you read **HEART-THROB** by Doris Parmett, LOVESWEPT #388. Hannah Morgan was bright, eager, beautiful—an enigma who filled television director Zack Matthews with impatience . . . and a sizzling hunger. The reporter in him wanted to uncover her mysteries, while the man simply wanted to gaze at her in moonlight. Hannah was prepared to work as hard as she needed to satisfy the workaholic heartbreaker . . . until her impossibly virile boss crumbled her defenses with tenderness and ignited a hunger she'd never expected to feel again. Was she

(continued)

willing to fight to keep her man? Don't miss this sparkling jewel of a love story. A true Valentine's Day present.

For a great finish to a special month, don't miss Judy Gill's **STARGAZER**, LOVESWEPT #389, a romance that shines with the message of the power of love . . . at any age. As the helicopter hovered above her, Kathy M'Gonigle gazed with wonder at her heroic rescuer, but stormy-eyed Gabe Fowler was furious at how close she'd come to drowning in the sudden flood—and shocked at the joy he felt at touching her again! Years before, he'd made her burn with desire, but she'd been too young and he too restless to settle down. Now destiny had brought them both home. Could the man who put the stars in her eyes conquer the past and promise her forever?

All our books—well, their authors wish they could promise you forever. That's not possible, but authors and staff can wish you wonderful romance reading.

Now it is my great pleasure to give you one more Valentine's gift—namely, to reintroduce you to our Susann Brailey, now Senior Editor, who will grace these pages in the future with her fresh and enthusiastic words. But don't think for a minute that you're getting rid of me! I'll be here—along with the rest of the staff—doing the very best to bring you wonderful love stories all year long.

As I have told you many times in the past, I wish you peace, joy, and the best of all things—the love of family and friends.

Carolyn Nichols

Carolyn Nichols
Editor
LOVESWEPT
Bantam Books
666 Fifth Avenue
New York, NY 10103

FAN OF THE MONTH

Joni Clayton

It's really great fun to be a LOVESWEPT Fan of the Month as it provides me with the opportunity to publicly thank Carolyn Nichols, Bantam Books, and some of my favorite authors: Sandra Brown, Iris Johansen, Kay Hooper, Fayrene Preston, Helen Mittermeyer and Deborah Smith (to name only a few!).

My good friend, Mary, first introduced me to romance fiction and LOVESWEPTS in 1984 as an escape from the pressures of my job. Almost immediately my associates noticed the difference in my disposition and attitude and questioned the reason for the change. They all wanted to thank LOVESWEPT!

It did not take me long to discover that most romance series were inconsistent in quality and were not always to my liking—but not LOVESWEPT. I have thoroughly enjoyed each and every volume. All were "keepers" . . . so of course I wanted to own the entire series. I enlisted the aid of friends and used book dealers. Presto! The series was complete! As soon as LOVESWEPT was offered through the mail, I subscribed and have never missed a copy!

I have since retired from the "hurly-burly" of the working world and finally have the time to start to reread all of my LOVESWEPT "keepers."

To Carolyn, all of the authors, and the LOVESWEPT staff—Thanks for making my retirement so enjoyable!

60 Minutes to a Better, More Beautiful You!

Now it's easier than ever to awaken your sensuality, stay slim forever—even make yourself irresistible. With Bantam's bestselling subliminal audio tapes, you're only 60 minutes away from a better, more beautiful you!

__ 45004-2	**Slim Forever**	$8.95
__ 45112-X	**Awaken Your Sensuality**	$7.95
__ 45081-6	**You're Irresistible**	$7.95
__ 45035-2	**Stop Smoking Forever**	$8.95
__ 45130-8	**Develop Your Intuition**	$7.95
__ 45022-0	**Positively Change Your Life**	$8.95
__ 45154-5	**Get What You Want**	$7.95
__ 45041-7	**Stress Free Forever**	$7.95
__ 45106-5	**Get a Good Night's Sleep**	$7.95
__ 45094-8	**Improve Your Concentration**	$7.95
__ 45172-3	**Develop A Perfect Memory**	$8.95

Bantam Books, Dept. LT, 414 East Golf Road, Des Plaines, IL 60016

Please send me the items I have checked above. I am enclosing $_____ (please add $2.00 to cover postage and handling). Send check or money order, no cash or C.O.D.s please. (Tape offer good in USA only.)

Mr/Ms _____

Address _____

City/State _____ Zip _____

LT-12/89

Please allow four to six weeks for delivery.
Prices and availability subject to change without notice.

THE DELANEY DYNASTY

Men and women whose loves an passions are so glorious
it takes many great romance novels by three bestselling
authors to tell their tempestuous stories.

THE SHAMROCK TRINITY

☐ 21975 RAFE, THE MAVERICK
by Kay Hooper $2.95

☐ 21976 YORK, THE RENEGADE
by Iris Johansen $2.95

☐ 21977 BURKE, THE KINGPIN
by Fayrene Preston $2.95

THE DELANEYS OF KILLAROO

☐ 21872 ADELAIDE, THE ENCHANTRESS
by Kay Hooper $2.75

☐ 21873 MATILDA, THE ADVENTURESS
by Iris Johansen $2.75

☐ 21874 SYDNEY, THE TEMPTRESS
by Fayrene Preston $2.75

THE DELANEYS: *The Untamed Years*

☐ 21899 GOLDEN FLAMES *by Kay Hooper* $3.50
☐ 21898 WILD SILVER *by Iris Johansen* $3.50
☐ 21897 COPPER FIRE *by Fayrene Preston* $3.50

Buy them at your local bookstore or use this page to order.

Bantam Books, Dept. SW7, 414 East Golf Road, Des Plaines, IL 60016

Please send me the items I have checked above. I am enclosing $_____
(please add $2.00 to cover postage and handling). Send check or money
order, no cash or C.O.D.s please.

Mr/Ms _____

Address _____

City/State _____ Zip _____

SW7–11/89

Please allow four to six weeks for delivery.
Prices and availability subject to change without notice.

NEW!

Handsome Book Covers Specially Designed To Fit Loveswept Books

Our new French Calf Vinyl book covers come in a set of three great colors—royal blue, scarlet red and kachina green.

Each 7" × 9½" book cover has two deep vertical pockets, a handy sewn-in bookmark, and is soil and scratch resistant.

To order your set, use the form below.